I0691410

A Shooting at Auke Bay Alaska Assassin: Crime, Collusion, Conspiracy

Gordon Parker
Tales of Crime and Corruption Creator

PUBLICATION
CONSULTANTS
We Believe In The Power Of Authors

PO Box 221974 Anchorage, Alaska 99522-1974

books@publicationconsultants.com, www.publicationconsultants.com

ISBN Number: 978-1-59433-881-6
eBook ISBN Number: 978-1-59433-882-3
Library of Congress Catalog Card Number: 2019942424

Dedicated to my son,

David,
who read every revision of every draft of every book.

I acknowledge others who read early drafts and offered encouragement, including Paul Rich, Tom Brenan, Rich Listowski, Kimberly Rimert (self-proclaimed #1 fan of Trent & Darcey), Don Cartee, Donn & Karen Wonnell, and Walt Larson (aka Ed Riley). My Thanks also to Willie Hensley who guided me to the perfect publisher and to Evan Swensen for having faith in me.

July 8ᵗʰ

Trent Marshall must die.

To see him here was to portend approaching disaster.

To let him live was to invite it.

The man had known that for more than a month. He had used the time to plan carefully.

From where he lay hidden in the trees, he had a clear view straight to the *Nanuq*, the luxury yacht tied up in the harbor at Auke Bay just outside of Juneau. The Schmidt & Bender scope was so precise he could have been on the *Nanuq's* aft deck.

When he awoke this morning, Trent Marshall didn't know the beautiful Southeast Alaska summer day would bring an existential crisis. It would not be a crisis of any length. Once Marshall stepped onto the deck and appeared in the circle of the scope, there would be only seconds of his life remaining.

The yacht was half a mile away. No challenge for the Remington Modular Sniper Rifle the man held steadily trained on the vessel. Resting on its bipod, the rifle had an effective range of almost a mile. At half that distance the .338 magnum slug would easily accomplish its assignment.

With the rifle's superior sound and flame suppressors, the shooter would not be spotted. Anyone watching would see only Marshall dying.

There was no emotion in the pending assassination. He was not stirred by what he was about to do. The man didn't dislike Marshall. He actually admired what the retired investigative reporter had accomplished in San Francisco four years prior. In a sense he was indebted to Marshall for taking down the alliance of four powerful criminal entities. He had been underboss and consigliere to the organizer and administrator of the federation. It was in the destruction of the alliance and its members that the man had found opportunity.

But admiration wouldn't save Marshall. This was business. Nothing more. Trent Marshall must die.

The man had known he must kill Marshall since the day he received the call from one of the sources he was careful to maintain in San Francisco. The source told him that Marshall had chartered a luxury yacht for a cruise up through the islands and fjords of the Alexander Archipelago, which made up Southeast Alaska.

The source thought Seattle was the yacht's home port.

The *Nanuq*. He was familiar with the vessel. He knew quite a lot about the *Nanuq*. It was important that he know everything about the yacht.

A week before Marshall and his family were to set sail, the man flew to Seattle. He spent two days wandering around the waterfront. He spotted the *Nanuq* right away. It was an impressive vessel. 120 feet long with six luxurious guest staterooms plus quarters for Captain Eric Hannigan and his wife, Sally, who was also chief stewardess. The first officer, chief engineer, bosun, a deck hand, a chef and a steward made up the rest of the crew.

The man figured chartering the *Nanuq* for a cruise through Southeast Alaska cost what most people would consider a fortune. Trent Marshall could afford it. As an investigative reporter he didn't make a lot of money, even after he won a Pulitzer Prize. Then his last living relative, his mother's aunt, died leaving him 1,000 acres of land just across the river from Baton Rouge. He and a partner built a golf course surrounded by scores of multi-million dollar homes. He invested his substantial profit from that venture wisely. Trent now counted his millions by hundreds.

The man observed the crew's routine carefully. The deck hand, he thought, offered the most potential for his purpose. Each evening the hand left the vessel headed for the Caduceous, a dive bar attempting sophistication in the choice of its name. Symbol of the messenger of the Greek gods; conductor of the dead; protector of merchants and thieves. The man found the deck hand sitting at the bar. He took the next stool.

The man was generous with drinks. The deck hand was thirsty. It didn't take long to learn the plan for the *Nanuq*'s upcoming cruise. A

6

few more drinks and the deck hand was convinced that a firm friendship had been formed. Money exchanged hands on the second night. On the third night, the deck hand agreed to call the man whenever the *Nanuq* was within range of a mobile tower. The man would know where Marshall was at all times.

The number the deck hand was given rang on a burner, a mobile phone bought at a convenience store. It couldn't be traced and when his business with the deck hand was done, the man would toss it into the ocean.

Activity on the *Nanuq's* aft deck brought him back to the present. But it was only the steward bringing out refreshments in preparation for the five o'clock cocktail hour. Based on his knowledge of Marshall's tastes, the man assumed the three bottles of red wine would be very good Napa Merlot. There was also an assortment of what appeared to be soft drinks. When the steward went back into the main cabin, the man relaxed, though he kept his eye on the scope.

The door to the main cabin opened again. This time a giggling three year old girl ran onto the deck pursued by two older women, one white, one black. The man knew that Betty Anderson was the mother of Darcey Anderson, Trent's wife. The black woman was Ivy Ford, who had been a friend to Trent's mother. Ivy became a mentor to the young white woman when they worked together at New Orleans' venerable Coffee Pot restaurant.

When his mother died unexpectedly, Ivy became a surrogate mother for the teenaged Trent, a relationship encouraged by Trent's father after the boy went to live with him in Baton Rouge. The father made sure Trent visited Ivy often at her New Orleans home.

After Trent and Darcey were married, Ivy remained an important part of their family. When Ivy's husband, Walter, passed away two years earlier, Darcey convinced the older woman it was time for her to retire. Trent converted the carriage house at his New Orleans home into an apartment for her.

The child was Kelli Elizabeth Ivy Marshal. She was named for Trent's mother, Darcey's mother who was called Betty, and the black woman who was there for Trent when little Kelli's grandmother died.

Now young Kelli was scampering around the deck. The women pretended they couldn't catch her. It was a happy game of chase with the child.

A younger woman, who the man knew to be Darcey Anderson, stepped into view. She sat next to the table on which the refreshments were arrayed, pleased to enjoy her daughter's play with the older women.

The steward reappeared to open a bottle of wine. He poured two glasses and, after speaking with the guests, began to open bottles of soft drinks and pour them into glasses filled with ice, including one sippy cup.

At last the target appeared. Trent Marshall stepped onto the deck. The child dropped her sippy cup and ran to him, leaping into his arms. He watched through the scope as Marshall swung his daughter around and around while Darcey picked up the cup. He couldn't hear what they were saying but he could imagine the words from the look on their faces.

It was too complicated. Too many people. Marshall was moving too much with his daughter. The man's job today was all business. Nothing else. He had no intention of killing anyone not connected with that business. Certainly not a child. The man might be cold and merciless. He didn't consider himself to be a monster.

He watched as Marshall turned to the pier in response to an activity not in the scope's view. He swung the rifle around until another man came into view walking down the pier. His snow white hair proved him to be elderly. Late seventies. Maybe eighties. He looked to be in relatively good shape for his age. He held a duffel bag in place on his shoulder with his left hand while he waved toward the boat with his right.

Another complication, the man thought.

Patience. Patience. The deck would clear at some point. There would be a safe shot. Patience.

The old man climbed aboard, dropping the duffel as Marshall embraced him. Marshall introduced the newcomer to the three women and then to the child, who converted quickly from giggling little girl to polite young lady. The man forced himself to push that sort of thought from his head. This was business. It wasn't helpful to put personalities together with faces.

Trent poured his guest a glass of wine. The man watched through the scope as they talked animatedly. He saw Darcey laugh. Trent and the newcomer were telling stories of adventures long past.

The man continued watching without impatience. He had all the time he needed. Daylight went long into the evening at this time of year in Southeast Alaska.

"Dad met Robert the first time he came to Alaska to work. I wasn't with him on that trip. Robert was chief of police in Anchorage in those days. Later he went on to command the State Troopers and finally wound up in the governor's cabinet as Commissioner of Public Safety," Marshall was explaining to Darcey.

"Now, Trent," the old man scolded, "you make it sound like I was important. I've never been anything but a cop, Darcey. Now I'm an old cop."

"Don't you believe it," Trent responded. "Robert Monk is a legend in Alaska. His hair might be white and there's not as much of it these days, but when he speaks Alaskans respond."

"None of that matters," Monk waved Trent's praise away. "What is important is your dad and I became good friends. And when the work here ended, he would bring you to Juneau for a few days each year. We had some great times out on the water. We caught a lot of salmon and halibut. And we had some good hunting trips."

"We always stayed at Robert's house, Darcey," Trent said, excitedly. "He's got this old house on Basin Road at the top of Starr Hill. The view from his living room is spectacular. The road leaves town not far past his house but it's an easy hike around Mount Juneau to the old Perseverance Mine. I had a great time exploring the mine shaft."

"Yeah, and you about scared the life out of your daddy and me. That old shaft was dangerous. Still is."

"Wasn't the first time I scared my dad," Trent said with a chuckle. "Robert also has the best library I've ever seen, Darcey. An entire room with bookshelves on all four walls, all filled. I can still recall the unique smell of old books. It's enough to bring on bibliosmia."

The old man laughed. "I think you read your way through most of them. And you picked up quite a vocabulary while you were doing it."

Monk had no children. He had never married. He told Trent's dad that he was married to the police force. And he said he found it difficult to think about strapping on a gun to go to work, not knowing if he would live through the day, leaving a family also not knowing.

Darcey set her empty wine glass on the table and stood to chase Kelli down.

"You two get caught up while Mom and Ivy and I get this little urchin cleaned up and presentable for dinner," she said. She kissed Trent before turning to chase a giggling little Kelli into the main cabin, followed by the two grandmotherly women, leaving the two men alone.

It was the moment the man a half mile away was waiting for. He had held Marshall in his scope through the arrival of the unexpected guest. The Schmidt & Bender was a fine instrument. He had made the adjustments on the scope for windage and elevation. He had also adjusted the ring on the scope to account for the parallax, the slight difference between his eye on the scope and the target over the half mile between them.

On deck Trent refilled their wine glasses.

"We're having red beans and rice for dinner, Robert," Trent informed his guest. "We've eaten so much seafood in the past week I requested some Louisiana country food. And Ivy gave the chef her own recipe so he'd get it right."

The man squeezed the trigger. There was a soft whisper of sound and the .338 bullet sped from the barrel on its way to the target. He estimated the missile's velocity at about 2,500 feet per second. That meant it would strike Marshall less than two seconds after leaving the barrel.

Monk was taking a sip of his wine when he was shocked to see a nasty red blotch appear on the right side of Trent's head. The blow of the bullet knocked Trent backwards in his chair, landing on the deck.

His eye still pressed to the scope, the man saw the red spot appear on Marshall's head. Saw him fall backwards onto the deck.

Immediately the man saw two other actions in quick succession. The first was the old man moving surprisingly quicker than would be expected for a man his age. He covered Marshall's body with his own. At the same time, he pulled up the right leg of his pants to draw a small semiautomatic weapon from an ankle holster.

The second sight was an unexpected bonus. The deck hand stepped into sight in the bow, oblivious to anything happening aft. The man had planned on getting rid of his spy aboard the *Nanuq* but didn't think the opportunity would come today. He wasted no time working the bolt action to move a new cartridge into firing position as he repositioned the rifle to follow the welcome target. Waiting for the moment.

When the hand reached the aft deck, he stopped to stare in shock at the sight of Trent Marshall's body lying on his overturned chair, blood streaming from his head. An old man covered Trent's body with his own, his small but effective Glock 27 swinging from side to side as he searched for the source of the bullet.

The man with the rifle squeezed the trigger a second time. The bullet struck the deck hand square in the back of his head, shattering his brain stem. The man thought he had made a good hit on Marshall. He had no doubt about the deck hand.

After picking up the used cartridge from the first shot to be discarded later, he began breaking down his rifle. He didn't hurry. But he wasted no time. His movements were measured and practiced. He disconnected the bipod. Flipped the release to fold the stock. Removed the scope as well as the sound and flame suppressor. He placed the rifle and its ancillary parts into the case made especially for it.

He carefully moved back into the spruce trees until he was certain he was out of sight of anyone. He walked casually to where he had left his minivan parked on the edge of the evergreens that grew along Fritz Cove Road.

As the man drove calmly away unnoticed in the light gray vehicle, the *Nanuq*'s aft deck was alive with activity. Ivy was in the galley with the chef keeping an eye on his execution of one her special recipes. The chef both resented having her in his galley and appreciated the learning opportunity.

They saw movement when Trent was slammed to the deck but didn't realize what had happened. The chef understood without question what was happening when the deck hand was shot. He immediately reached for the vessel's phone and called up to the bridge.

Though he was stung with disbelief that a passenger and member of his crew had been shot on his vessel, Captain Hannigan instinctively

11

reached into a locker to retrieve a large, semiautomatic hand gun with dual barrels, the only weapon he allowed on board.

Alerted by the sound of critical activity, Darcey came out of her stateroom in time to see the captain racing aft, his bulky handgun at the ready, shouting for Ivy and the chef to stay down. Alarmed, she followed quickly behind him.

As the captain moved cautiously onto the open deck, Darcey came to a shocked standstill. She saw her husband lying on the deck, Robert Monk protecting him with his own body. For a moment she was unable to move. Unable to make a sound. Suspended in disbelief.

The sound of her curious daughter brought her back to dreaded reality. She shouted to Betty take Kelli into one of the staterooms. The child's grandmother didn't know what had happened. But she rushed to comply with daughter's shouted direction. Looking over her shoulder as she shooed Kelli back into the state room, Betty's worried eyes followed Darcey as she ran toward where Trent lay on the deck.

Ivy rose from where the chef had pulled her to the floor to keep her from danger. She saw Trent lying motionless on the deck, blood streaming from his head.

"Oh, no," she cried out, tears running from her eyes. "My boy. My boy. They've killed my boy."

Darcey was now running on adrenaline. She had to keep the others under control so she could save her husband.

"Ivy, go help Mom with Kelli," she called out. "That's what Trent needs you to do now."

Ivy wiped her eyes with a paper towel the chef handed to her. Still crying and grief stricken, she turned to do as Darcey ordered.

Darcey knelt by her husband, cradling his bloody head. The captain had placed himself, with his imposing weapon between the other three and the vessel's gunwales. He had already determined that his deck hand was dead. He wasn't sure about Trent.

Monk was on the phone issuing orders to someone. Whoever was on the other end of the call was apparently obeying.

"A helicopter is on its way. Juneau cops and State Troopers, too," Monk said, as he ended the call. "How's he doing?"

Darcey felt numb. She couldn't cry. She could only hold her husband's head, his blood staining her clothing.

"He's still breathing," she said.

"The helicopter will get him to the hospital here," Monk said.

"And then what?" Darcey asked, in a monotone.

"I don't know," Monk replied honestly. "Either they'll take care of him here or we'll medevac him to Anchorage. A medevac jet is already in the air from Anchorage. It'll be here in less than an hour and a half. By then we'll know if we need it or not."

The man drove south on Fritz Cove Road. He first heard, then saw the helicopter on its way to the boat harbor. It was a medevac chopper. They wouldn't be looking for him.

As he turned onto Engineers Cutoff Road he heard the sirens of multiple police vehicles. He followed that road north toward Glacier Highway.

He thought the police would set up a road block closer to the harbor. They would be looking for someone driving away from the scene. He turned west on Glacier Highway, driving toward the harbor.

He encountered the first of numerous police near the northern end of Fritz Cove Road where it intersected with Glacier Highway near the campus of the University of Alaska Southeast. There were only a few vehicles on the road. He was the only one headed toward Auke Bay. The others had been on their way into Juneau when they were stopped.

A young woman in the distinctive blue State Trooper uniform with a gold stripe running down the leg and matching corporal's stripes on her sleeve motioned for the man to stop. He did so without hesitation and with no negative reaction as the officer approached his minivan.

"Can I see some identification, sir?" she requested, politely but with a tone that said refusal wouldn't be the correct response.

"Certainly, corporal," the man said as he reached into his hip pocket for his wallet. He handed his Alaska driver's license to her.

She looked the license over carefully before handing it back to him.

"Thank you, Mr. Segal," she said. "May I ask your business in Auke Bay today?'

13

Jim Segal hadn't always been his name. When Pietro, or sometimes Peter, Greco purchased a new identify in preparation for abandoning San Francisco, it came with that name. It also said he was born in Homer, Alaska. When the skipper of the yacht taking him out of San Francisco Bay asked for the course he should set, Greco thought, "Why not?"

"North," he replied. "Set our course to north."

And he became Jim Segal.

Before he could answer a cop in the similar though darker blue of the local Juneau police department walked up.

"It's ok, Susan," Officer Barlow King assured his colleague. "Jim's ok. He's the guy who's opening the new restaurant down on South Franklin Street across from where the cruise ships dock. This is Corporal Susan Duryea, Jim. She's a good cop."

"Nice to meet you, Corporal," Segal said. "What's going on? This looks serious."

"Looks like there's been shooting, sir. Couple of guys are reported down on a yacht in the harbor."

"That's awful," Segal said. Outwardly sympathetic. Inwardly pleased. "I'm sorry to hear it. It's terrible that some people can be so feckless, especially with guns."

"This isn't just someone being irresponsible, Jim," King interjected. "Looks like it might have been planned. No one saw the shooter or even where the shots came from."

"That's even worse. Certainly not something this community is used to." Turning back to the State Trooper he continued, "In answer to your question, as Barlow said I'm opening a new restaurant soon. JS Bistro Southeast. I was just driving out to see if there were any fishermen around. Trying to set up as many local suppliers as I can get. But it looks like this is not a good time. I think I'll just turn around, if it's ok with you, and head back to town."

"Probably a good idea, sir," the corporal responded.

"Nice to meet you, Corporal," Segal said.

"My pleasure, sir."

"Barlow, let's have coffee soon. It's your turn to buy," he called out as he maneuvered his minivan through a U-turn.

14

King responded with an affirmative wave.

Segal liked King. The cop really believed that most people don't lie and cheat and steal and kill. Segal thought the cop naïve. He hoped he wouldn't have to kill him some day.

Dr. Younger found Darcey and Monk in the hospital's family waiting room. Darcey looked at him anxiously. She was afraid to hear what he was about to say. She reached for Robert's hand.

"The good news is Mr. Marshall is stabilized. His vital signs are weak but steady," the doctor reported.

"Will he live?" she asked, dreading the answer.

Dr. Younger paused before answering.

"I don't know, Ms. Anderson. He has a chance but I don't know. He has a brain injury. It's not the worst I've ever seen but it's still a blow to his brain. The most difficult injury to treat. The most difficult to survive. He has to have surgery and the sooner the better."

"Can it be done here? Can you do it?" Darcey asked, her voice trembling with fear.

"This is a good hospital, Ms. Anderson, with competent doctors and staff. But I'm not a brain surgeon and neither are my colleagues. His best chance is for us to medevac him to Anchorage. There are excellent surgeons there who specialize in brain injuries. We need to get him there now."

"I ordered a medevac plane down from Anchorage while we were still waiting for the chopper," Robert said. "It's here now, refueled and ready to take him to Anchorage."

Dr. Younger nodded. "We'll get him ready to travel," he said as he headed back to the emergency room where Trent lay unconscious but breathing.

Robert took Darcey's hands in his.

"He's strong, Darcey. He's going to make it. We have to believe that. And you're every bit as strong as he is. I know that. He's told me about the scrapes the two of you have been in together. I know about the time in Louisiana when you used a pretty little nickel plated .38 single action revolver to take down the lunatic who kidnapped your mother and him. And when you went after the Mafia soldier in San Francisco who kidnapped you and your business partner. You chased that guy into the ocean with an M16. Anybody can handle a .38 revolver. But an M16 is a powerful automatic rifle. Takes some gumption to handle one of those."

"This might sound silly, Robert, but those things seem easy now," she said, wiping away tears with a tissue, her eyes lowered. "I could do something in both those situations. This time I feel helpless."

"And that's when you have to get even tougher, Darcey," Robert said. "That's when you have to get just plain mean. You never give up, Darcey. Never give up."

She nodded, raising her eyes to look Monk full in the face.

"You're right, Robert. So what do I do?"

"Right now you get on that flight with Trent. Just be with him. He'll know you're with him and knowing that is the best medicine he can have right now."

"All right. But what about Kelli and Mom and Ivy? And what are you going to do?"

Robert had planned on joining them on the *Nanuq* to cruise up to Glacier Bay, then across the northern edge of the Gulf of Alaska, and through Prince William Sound to Whittier. From there they had planned to take the train to Anchorage.

"I'll go back to Auke Bay and help them pack up. I don't think it would be a good idea for them to spend the night on the yacht and I doubt if we have time to catch an evening flight. They can spend the night at my house. I have lots of room and I can protect them there. There's a nonstop flight that leaves here around 1:30 tomorrow afternoon and arrives in Anchorage about three o'clock. I'll book all four of us on that."

"When you get to Anchorage, I guess we can talk about how to find out who did this."

"You bet we will," he said. "I still have some influence with cops in Alaska. And if we need the governor, I know him, too. Oh, and you might want to just check into the Captain Cook Hotel when you get there. You can pick up a few things you need in their sundry store. Hopefully we can get into the condo Trent rented a few days early."

"I'm going to be at the hospital most of the time," she replied, with determination.

"Well, you have to rest. You're not going to do Trent any good if you're worn out and get sick yourself."

"Thanks, Robert," Darcey said, giving him a kiss on the cheek. "You're really very sweet."

Monk grunted.

"Huh. I'm just a curmudgeonly old cop who doesn't like it when someone shoots one of my pals."

Darcey started to leave, then turned back.

"Uh, Robert, about packing up our things…"

"Yes?"

"There's something you should know," she said, haltingly.

"How big and what caliber?" he asked.

"Trent has a reproduction of his LeMat revolver."

"Nine .44 caliber balls and a second unrifled barrel bored for twenty gauge shot. Cap and ball, black powder handgun. Considered a collector's item in Alaska. Not a problem," he said. "And you?"

"A single shot .410 hand gun with a ten inch barrel," she said quietly.

The old man shook his head. He looked thoughtfully out the window. He shook his head but he was smiling when he looked back at Darcey.

"Well, I became acculturated to the world of Trent Marshall and his rules that don't always match everyone else's a long time ago. That weapon has been completely illegal since passage of the National Firearms Act in 1934. It presents more of a problem. But I'll figure something out."

"I have the papers that Trent's great uncle got when he registered it during the 1968 amnesty. The gun is in a box in my suitcase and the registration is with it," she offered.

"That should do the trick. Now get in there with Trent. Don't worry about anything here. We'll catch up to you tomorrow."

Jim Segal was on time to catch the evening flight to Anchorage. He had stopped by the apartment over the building he was renovating to hide the rifle in a secret compartment he had built in the bedroom closet.

He really did intend to open a restaurant in Juneau. It would be the companion to his highly successful JS Bistro in Anchorage. But it wasn't the main business he intended for Southeast Alaska.

When Trent and Darcey, along with their colleagues, Detective Sergeants Christopher Booth and Nancy Patrick, had launched Operation Den of Snakes to take down the alliance of four criminal organizations in San Francisco, Segal immediately realized how vulnerable the fragile relationship among the four gangs was. And he saw opportunity.

He acted quickly to betray and assassinate his boss, Jonathan Rossi, head of the Rossi Mafia family and the man who had organized the alliance. He then methodically, and personally, did away with the leaders of the three remaining groups. After eliminating all four he confiscated stashes of emergency funds each had kept in his office as well as the money Rossi kept in a safe deposit box. He had been foolish enough to allow his consigliere to access it. Altogether it amounted to a substantial sum.

Segal also stole the yacht of his last victim, an $8 million vessel that he gave to its captain, Gary Place, thereby gaining the seaman's lifelong loyalty. Captain Place quickly registered the vessel, which he renamed Dancer, in a friendly country whose government didn't ask any questions.

Segal arrived in Alaska with several millions. He had no need to work and for a while did nothing but tour the land of Jim Segal's birth. He opened JS Bistro out of boredom, hiring the best chef and staff he could find. JS Bistro was an immediate success. He enjoyed playing host to the elite of Anchorage, all of whom were anxious for the company of this native of Alaska who had returned home after finding success in other parts of the world.

Eventually even that began to bore him. While his restaurant was successful it was, of course, the liquor license that brought the money pouring in. A liquor license, he knew, could be very helpful when it came to sliding illicit money into the legal economy.

Then he read an article about a smuggling industry that was making billions for those with the brains and guts to get into it. While live streaming of concerts and movies made a difference, there was still a healthy market for counterfeit CDs and movies. The market became even larger when counterfeit jewelry, fashion, video games, pharmaceuticals, and other products were added. And there was always the possibility of occasionally hijacking a load of weapons headed for a military base or a border patrol unit.

He remembered the many small bays and inlets he had seen in Southeast Alaska. Given Alaska's strategic location between Asia and North America, Southeast Alaska seemed to him designed with smugglers in mind. He went to work.

It didn't take long for him to make contact with suppliers in Asia who could provide the counterfeit products. He got in touch with some of his old cohorts in the continental U.S. and Mexico to talk about guns. He stayed away from street drugs. There were too many people already in that market, most of whom seemed to wind up either dead or in jail on a regular basis. Neither fate interested him.

He enlisted Captain Place with Dancer. Place located three other vessels with greedy owners. All three were larger and slower than Dancer. They could carry more cargo and if they got caught it wouldn't be a problem for Segal. Captain Place might have to stay out of sight for a while but nothing more than that.

On the recommendation of a San Francisco friend, he brought in Cameron McGraw to oversee the Southeast operation. McGraw was from the east coast and had some experience in the restaurant business. His public job would be manager of JS Bistro Southeast. Privately he would be busy with other things.

Monk and Captain Hannigan sat in the main cabin while Sally Hannigan and the steward assisted the women with the packing. Hannigan was still in a stage of disbelief that such a thing could have happened on his vessel. Monk tried to encourage him to talk his way out of his state of shock.

"That looked like one monster of a weapon you hit the deck with, Captain," the old cop said.

Hannigan had stuck the hand gun in his belt once it was clear the shooting was over. Now he laid it on the table where the two men sat. Monk picked it up and looked it over.

"An Arsenal Firearms double barreled 1911," Monk said. "I've heard about it but never saw one before. I also heard there are some problems with it."

"Yeah, it's not the most effective weapon," the captain agreed. "It's basically two 1911s stuck together. Two of everything. It's not accurate at any distance. One bullet will go straight to the target but the other will waiver off. It's also too bulky and the slide is very difficult to work. But if you're close enough to your target and only have to fire once it's ok. Plus there's the psychological factor. Like a double barrel shotgun.

19

Point that thing at a bad guy who doesn't know much about guns and it'll scare the pants off him."

Monk laughed. "That's not a bad theory."

The steward enlisted the bosun to help load the luggage into Monk's SUV. He thanked them, then rose and shook hands with the captain.

"I'll talk to Darcey tomorrow about settling accounts with you."

"Don't worry about that," the captain responded. "Trent paid a considerable cash deposit up front plus we have his credit card on file. We'll figure it out. Just take care of Trent."

The chef came over with a tightly covered pot.

"You'll need to eat, Mr. Monk," he said. "This is the pot of red beans I prepared using Mrs. Ford's recipe. Cooking some rice and cornbread will help keep the ladies' minds occupied with something other than the shooting."

"Thanks, Chef. That's very thoughtful of you. Much appreciated."

Later in the evening Monk sipped a martini as he stared out the large window of his home overlooking Juneau, Gastineau Channel, and Douglas Island. Betty and Ivy had taken Kelli upstairs where all three were in bed. Kelli loved the idea of spending the night at Monk's house and thought the view splendid. It helped get her mind off her daddy.

Monk was thinking about Jim Segal. As he drove back to Auke Bay, he had seen Segal turn into the airport with his man McGraw driving him. Probably going to catch the evening flight to Anchorage.

As far as he knew Segal was a successful business man. Nothing more. Still there was something about him that set Monk's cop antennae buzzing. He had only talked with the man twice. When he asked where Segal had worked before he retired and came back to Alaska, the answer was equivocal. It wasn't much. Just enough to make Monk wonder.

He was also curious about McGraw. The Irishman was not especially friendly. He had a hard look about him.

He also knew that whenever Segal was in Southeast, he and McGraw spent a lot of time exploring the fjords and islands in a boat Segal kept at Aurora Basin harbor. A Sea Ray Sundancer. Very nice boat.

He rented a slip with a stall, which he kept locked. But then lots of people did that. They were after fish. Segal probably was, too, though some of Monk's buddies mentioned that he hardly ever came into the harbor with a catch.

Like Trent, Monk didn't believe in coincidence. In fact, Trent learned that from the experienced lawman. He knew Segal was renovating a building that would house a restaurant so he had reason to be in town. Still he was here on the day that Trent was shot. And he never seemed to catch fish.

Monk knew he was being unfair. He had no reason to suspect Segal of anything.

Just instinct.

But he didn't believe in coincidence.

July 9th

Darcey sat across the desk from Dr. Natalie Shannon. She knew the doctor was tired. She had been working to save Trent's life since nine o'clock the previous night. It was now three o'clock in the morning.

Darcey was desperate to know if Trent had a chance to live. She was afraid to ask. She waited to hear what Dr. Shannon had to say.

"First, Ms. Anderson, your husband is alive," she said.

Darcey felt the rush of relief flow through her.

"Thank God," she said. "And thank you, Doctor."

"You can also thank whoever shot him," the doctor said. "He was good but not good enough. The distance was great and Trent was moving just enough to avoid a killing shot."

"Will he survive, Doctor? And if he does, will there be any lasting damage?"

"I don't know the answer to either yet. He received what we call a perforating wound, meaning the bullet didn't lodge in the brain but passed through the right frontal lobe tip. It didn't pass through any vital brain tissue or vascular structures.

"The right side of the brain is popularly known as the creative side. It allows us to visualize through feeling rather than thought. It's our artistic side. The left side of the brain is the part that allows us to think in words, consider facts and math and logic."

"So Trent's speech and ability to think shouldn't be impaired?" Darcey asked.

"If we're lucky," Dr. Shannon hesitated before continuing, "And if he survives. But it'll be a while before we know either. For the next three days our biggest concern will be swelling in his brain. We removed a small piece of his skull both to assess the damage and to relieve pressure for the inevitable swelling.

"Now I'm going to get some sleep. And you need to rest, too. If he survives, Trent is going to have to lean on you during his recovery. We can't have you getting sick."

"Can I see him?"

"Yes, but only through the window. A portion of his brain is exposed. It's critical that we maintain a sterile environment around him," she said. She again paused for a moment before adding, "If he is going to heal."

Darcey nodded, again feeling the tears welling up in her eyes. Dr. Shannon took notice.

"You must be exhausted," she said, "and it's late to try to find a hotel room. I can't let you be in the room with him but I can have a bed set up outside his window and put a screen around it. At least he'll be in your sight and maybe you can get a little sleep."

Darcey lay on the uncomfortable bed staring through the glass at her unconscious husband. Monk had called Anchorage Police Chief Benjamin Kline to request an undercover officer posted in the hospital and Dr. Shannon reluctantly agreed. They also asked Dr. Shannon to list him in the hospital records under an assumed name. The hospital management evidenced some nervousness about the unusual request but agreed after Chief Kline assured them he approved.

In Juneau, Monk made shrimp cakes for breakfast using the tiny Petersburg shrimp so plentiful in Southeast Alaska waters. Kelli was thrilled to help him in the kitchen. Her main job was to set the table and serve the cakes after each was covered with a fried egg.

Shortly after nine o'clock Darcey called. She had slept for five hours and was still tired. She told Monk what she had learned about Trent's condition.

"I'm relieved to hear he's hanging on, Darcey," the old man responded. "Let me suggest, however, that we not let the news of his survival be publicly known. It won't hurt to let our shooter think the assassination was successful."

He had already talked to the right people in Juneau to keep the story as quiet as possible. The cops had to tell the press something. They said only that a tourist and a deck hand had been shot. They were working on it but had no leads to report. And they were trying to reach the next of kin to notify them before releasing the victims' identities. The media lost interest quickly as the governor called the legislature back to town for the second special session of the year as the state's budget battles continued.

Darcey told Monk she had talked to the owners of the condo Trent had rented. They had no problem with the family moving in a few days early. She planned to get a rental car and pick up keys later in the morning. She would also lay in some groceries before meeting their flight in the afternoon.

"I think we should get Kelli, Betty, and Ivy out of the state as soon as possible. But I don't want to do that until we can be sure they're protected. I'm working on a plan," Monk said.

Jim Segal had slept well. He was pleased with the state of his world as he knew it. He left his home on Second Avenue in downtown Anchorage to walk the few blocks to Fifth Avenue and JS Bistro.

The lunch crowd was just beginning to wander in when he arrived. He took time to greet each of his guests as he always did. He was also careful to return all the greetings of his staff as he looked into the kitchen.

He noticed the young woman recently hired as a prep cook. She was thin. Maybe, he thought, it was just the way she dressed that made her appear so. Her hair was short with a black streak through the center and red stripes on the sides. It looked like she cut it herself. It was like she wanted to appear unattractive. Too bad. He thought she might be quite desirable if she wanted to be.

There was also something oddly familiar about her. He tried to remember her name. Florence or something similar?

Satisfied that the kitchen was running smoothly, he made his way to the stairs at the end of the bar. A landing at the top of the stairs opened to the right into a large room reserved for special events. It could be divided into smaller rooms as needed. The office he shared with his manager was to the left.

As usual, Jayne Colombo was working at her desk when he entered. She was an attractive woman, though her blonde hair and blue eyes belied her Italian heritage to some. He wasn't at all sure that the name she called herself was any more the one with which she was born than was Jim Segal his.

He knew her family came from Lombardy. Colombo is one of the most common family names in that northern region of Italy, which borders Switzerland. In fact, Lombardy was ruled by the French, Spanish, Austrians, and even many centuries ago, Germanic tribes longer than it has been part of Italy. In the 21st century Milan emerged as Italy's economic powerhouse. The industrious citizens of Milan don't always appreciate their southern neighbors.

He also knew she was as ruthless as was he. Anyone who stood in her way would likely wind up carrying several lumps of lead from the MAC 10 machine pistol of which she was fond and from which she was never separated. Small enough to fit in the large bag she always carried, its thirty round magazine of .45 ACP cartridges could blaze off at a rate of more than a thousand rounds per minute. But it was notoriously inaccurate. It had been said that it was good only if the fight was being waged inside an old-fashioned telephone booth.

Its saving grace was the revolutionary two-piece sound suppressor that was developed somewhere along the line as the Military Armaments Corporation tried to save its entry into the worldwide military market. That, and the fact that alluring aura emanating from her like the sweet fragrance of a frangipani flower made it easy to get most men and many women into the telephone booth with her.

Killing and sex were connected in some weird way for her. He learned that one night in San Francisco when he assigned her to a job. She met the target at his hotel. Two hours later she showed up at Segal's front door, face flushed and breathing heavily.

It was a memorable night. It was a disquieting night. He realized she was a psychopathic murderess. She could be useful if he could control her. That was the question. Could he control her? If she was caught carrying out an assignment, he could always say he was unaware that she was a serial killer.

He decided to risk it. But he would keep a close eye on her.

They trusted each other as much as two people in their world could trust. When he opened the restaurant, he brought her to Anchorage as his general manager. She was as efficient as she was remorseless. Those were the qualities he needed in his chief of staff. There would be things other than a restaurant to manage.

She looked up when he entered. Leaning back in her chair, she reached for the pack of Marlboros on her desk. Lighting one, she blew smoke through pouty lips before speaking.

"So how did it go in Juneau?" she asked.

"Couldn't be better. They got him to the hospital but I could see the head shot. He didn't look to have much life left in him, if any. Anything in the news here?"

"Not a word," she said. "But this isn't New Orleans or San Francisco. He's not well known here. He could die and the media wouldn't notice."

He sat down at his own desk across the room and starting going through the mail Jayne had left for him.

"That new prep cook we hired. The one with the weird hair. What's her name?"

Jayne laughed.

"She's kind of young, isn't she? Must be a middle-aged man thing."

Segal didn't mind being the source of her amusement. He smiled.

"Her name is Fiona Robinson. She's from somewhere back east. Just one of the kids who come through Alaska on their travels before they have to settle down. At least she's earning her keep instead of letting mommy and daddy pay her way. She's a good worker, too."

Segal let the subject drop. Business was more important.

"Dancer will be cruising north this evening to meet one of our friends from Asia," Segal said. "She'll return to the West Coast with a cargo of ladies' fashions and accessories. Prada handbags and shoes."

"Is he bringing any cargo for trade?"

"Nope. This one will be an all cash deal. But a good one," Segal said. "We pay ten bucks for a handbag, sell it for $700 and the customers won't ask any questions. As far as they know they're getting the real deal for a bargain basement price."

"Yeah, and hopefully the products won't fall apart before the customers get home with'em," Jayne added, mockingly.

Dancer would cruise slowly and be at the southern end of the Alexander Archipelago near Ketchikan sometime in the next couple of days. Captain Place had to avoid attracting undue attention to himself.

Place knew the strategy was to bluff if challenged by a cutter. If that didn't work, they would run and hope no one called in air power.

Dancer should be able to slip away. Their trading partners' vessel might not be as fast. To emphasize the strategy, Segal told Place the old Alaska joke about running into a bear.

"In that case, Place," he said, "I don't have to outrun the bear. I just have to outrun you."

Place got the point. He just had to outrun the larger ship delivering the counterfeit cargo. Better to lose a partner than the whole operation. Losing a ship was one of the costs of doing business for their Asian suppliers.

Place and the other skippers were instructed to do whatever they had to do to avoid a fight. That would bring too much attention. Attention was the last thing they needed.

"You should have let me do it," Jayne said.

Segal was puzzled by the non sequitur.

"Do what?"

"The hit. You should have let me do it," she repeated.

"Wouldn't have worked. You couldn't get Marshall alone. You would have had to get on the yacht. And if you did that, you'd have to kill everyone on board. That would have made too big a mess," he said. "No. This one had to be a long distance kill."

The girl with multi colored hair didn't look up as Segal walked through the kitchen. Nevertheless, she watched him from beneath lowered lashes as he strolled through the kitchen. She saw him looking at her. She didn't raise her eyes. She didn't want him to see the emotion that would be so obvious.

"We have to get Kelli, Betty, and Ivy to your New Orleans house," Monk was saying. "It seems the safest place for them with its protective brick wall blocking entry from the street."

They were in the sitting room of a large, four bedroom penthouse overlooking the Bootleggers Cove neighborhood in downtown Anchorage. It had magnificent views on three sides. Cook Inlet and Mount Susitna, known as the Sleeping Lady by locals, to the west with the Alaska Range far beyond, capped by the shining majesty of the mighty Denali anchoring the northern end. To the east, they looked over the city of Anchorage with its backdrop of the Chugach Mountain range.

"I'm not leaving Trent, Robert," Darcey said in a tone that made it clear it was not a point for discussion.

"I didn't expect you would, Darcey," the old man replied. "I'm not leaving either."

"Then how do we get them to New Orleans?"

With perfect timing, the buzzer sounded, indicating someone was in the lobby asking to be allowed upstairs.

"I think the answer has just arrived," Monk said.

James Hackett was a few years younger than Monk and looked to be in the same excellent physical condition. Monk and Hackett were partners during their time with the Anchorage Police Department. Hackett stayed with APD when Monk moved to the State Troopers. When he was appointed Commissioner of Public Safety for the state, Monk brought Hackett in as his deputy.

Hackett had been married but lost his wife to cancer several years earlier. It was a long, painful struggle for both of them. They had no children. Hackett took her death badly.

Now the two old cops had another joint assignment. To protect Trent Marshall's family.

At five o'clock, the cocktail hour religiously observed by Trent, Darcey mixed rum and cokes for herself, Robert, and James. They went out on the west deck overlooking Cook Inlet and the Sleeping Lady to continue their planning.

Kelli was in the kitchen happily assisting Betty and Ivy as they prepared dinner. They were letting ribeye steaks rest in Creole seasoning while they prepared rice seasoned with roasted red peppers, onion, garlic, turmeric, smoked paprika, cumin, and a pinch each of saffron and cinnamon. It was a Caribbean influenced dish that Ivy often made.

"We're up against a well organized enemy," Monk said. "I judge the shot that took Trent down was made from at least half a mile. That means the shooter has a very sophisticated weapon and knows how to use it. They're not easy to come by and they're not cheap."

"The rifle or the shooter?" Darcey asked.

"Both," was the answer.

Darcey looked out across the inlet at the Sleeping Lady. She considered Monk's words. She shivered. She was wearing a light jacket. It wasn't the cool air. It was fear. But she had long since learned not to let fear stop her. It wouldn't stop the people around her either.

"We're going to need more troops," she said.

"I'll get in touch with the Anchorage cops, State Troopers, and Department of Public Safety. We'll get them to help us or at least stay out of our way."

"Some of those guys are pretty territorial, Robert," Hackett spoke up. "They might not be cooperative."

"If I have to call the governor, I will," Monk said. "If we have to go around some of them, we know how to do that, too, James. And with you in New Orleans with Betty, Ivy, and Kelli, we won't have to worry about them."

Hackett nodded.

"I have a feeling that whoever is behind the attempt on Trent's life isn't a loner," Monk continued. "I think we have an organization that extends from Anchorage to Southeast Alaska, and maybe beyond."

Darcey turned her head to look at him. Then she looked at the park two blocks away. She studied the foliage there.

"We're going to need a lot more troops," she concluded.

Same Day. Dimension Unknown.

Trent was aware that Darcey had been there. He heard every word she and the doctor said as they stood outside his door.

He tried to talk to her but he couldn't speak. He wanted to see her but couldn't open his eyes. He could only lie there.

He wondered if this was what it's like being dead. Was he dead? It didn't seem logical. He was hooked up to machines. An IV in each arm. If this was death it was remarkubly similar to life after a really bad accident.

The worst was when he heard her say, "I love you, Trent Marshall. Please don't leave me."

He wanted to tell her he was still here. That he didn't want to leave her. That he wouldn't leave her if it was in his power to stay.

Stay where?

He didn't know where he was. His last memory was of having a glass of wine with Robert Monk on the aft deck of the Nanuq. He remembered a blow to the head. A strong blow to the head. Like being hit with a shovel. Or a bat.

Then he was in this hospital. Darcey was here. And he couldn't talk to her. Couldn't see her. He couldn't feel her lips kissing him.

He lay in the bed silently. He was aware only of...

Of what?

He was aware only of what? Of everything? Of nothing?

Of life? Of death? Of something in between?

July 10th

After her visit with Trent the night before, Darcey was able to sleep through the night. She awoke refreshed. Energized. Ready to fight.

It was Monday morning. There were travel arrangements to be made. And it was time to call in Trent's troops.

Half an hour later she was in the kitchen with Kelli making one of her daughter's favorite breakfasts. Scrambled eggs with stir fried zucchini and sausage. None of those fruit smoothie things for this three year old. She was, after all, Trent Marshall's daughter. Breakfast, in her pretty eyes, meant eggs and sausage. If Mommy wanted to add some healthy vegetables, that was ok, too.

After breakfast Kelli crawled up into her mommy's lap. Darcey told the child she got to go on a trip with Betty and Ivy, both of whom Kelli considered her grandmothers. They were going to take her to the New Orleans house for a few days.

That delighted Kelli. She loved the New Orleans house. Because the courtyard was protected from street traffic by the brick wall Kelli could play outside all by herself as much as she liked. The adults could easily keep an eye on her from the house.

The little girl asked her mommy when she would get there.

Darcey could only say, "Soon, sweetie, soon."

"Will Daddy be with you?" the little girl asked.

Darcey hesitated for only a moment before answering, with determination, "Yes, sweetie. Daddy will be with me."

She refused to believe anything less.

31

Darcey let Betty tend to getting Kelli dressed while she drove to the airport. Robert had called the chief executive officer of a company that owned a Gulfstream G450. While the aircraft was most often used to ferry executives and visiting VIPs to Alaska's energy rich North Slope or down to the continental U.S., the aircraft had also been loaned to law enforcement from time to time. The CEO didn't hesitate to accommodate Robert's request without asking any questions. He also agreed to meet Darcey at the airport to give her a personal tour of the airplane.

Darcey was pleased with what she saw. Designed to accommodate up to nineteen passengers, the aircraft offered plenty of space for the family of three and their guardian. With a full galley and crew, including a flight attendant who would provide meals and snacks, Kelli and her companions should be very comfortable. With a range of almost five thousand miles, the Gulfstream could easily make the flight to New Orleans without having to refuel.

Meanwhile, Robert was meeting with Anchorage Police Chief Ben Kline at APD headquarters on Elmore just south of Tudor Road. Hackett had returned early that morning to the condo and now was on duty there while Monk used his truck.

Kline looked tired.

"How did you do it, Robert?" Chief Kline asked.

"It has to be in your blood, Ben," was the answer. "That's the only way a cop survives."

"Oh, that part's easy," the chief responded. "It's the politics that get me. Some days I think about resigning and going back to the streets."

Robert laughed.

"I know that feeling all too well," the old man said. "And if you think it's bad behind that desk, try going to Juneau with Public Safety. The best days I had on that job was when I flew around the state to visit Trooper stations and local cops."

Robert briefed the chief on the events of the past couple of days. He outlined the plan they had put into place and asked for APD's cooperation.

"You have it, Robert," Kline agreed. "Whatever you need. I'll play my role and if there's any help you need from my department, you'll get it."

At Monk's request Chief Kline agreed to assign two cars to escort them to the airport the next day. Perhaps they were being overly cautious but better that, Monk thought, than putting Trent and Darcey's family in jeopardy.

"Oh, and one more thing, Ben," Monk said. "It would be good if your men didn't get too curious about what Hackett might have with him. He has a job to do and will need his tools."

Kline grinned. "My men wouldn't dream of separating a workman from his tools."

Monk's meeting with Major Dylan Loughlin, acting commander of the Alaska State Troopers, didn't go as well.

"I don't care what you've done in the past, Mr. Monk," the major said. "You're not in command of the State Troopers now. As far as I'm concerned, you're just another civilian. You do anything out of line and I'll come down on you as hard as I can."

Monk didn't give Loughlin the details of their plans. He would save that for the phone call he would make next. Hopefully he could at least keep the major from getting in their way.

He made the call from Hackett's truck. It was a more productive conversation. When Monk finished his briefing and reported on the different reactions from APD and the acting Trooper commander, there was a loud sigh on the other end of the line.

"That man wants a promotion and assignment as commander of the Troopers. He's not going to get it this way," was the response from Juneau. "I'll have a talk with the major. Just be careful, Robert. I'll back you up as far as I can. But don't push me, or the governor for that matter, into a corner. There's only so much we can do to protect you."

"Fair enough," Monk said.

In the afternoon, Darcey made several calls to San Francisco, New Orleans, and Sabine Parish, the rural area in northwest Louisiana where her mother lived at the Pines, the farm that had been in her family for more than 150 years. Trent's troops were gathering.

Christopher Booth, now a captain in the San Francisco Police Department, and his partner, Nancy Patrick, still a sergeant in the suburban Richmond PD and not happy about it, both agreed to fly north in answer

Darcey's call for help. She told them to be ready to leave within the next day or two, if that worked for them. She would make the travel arrangements.

Sabine Parish Sheriff Jack Blake and New Orleans Police Captain Jordan Baron also insisted on coming to Alaska. Darcey thanked them but asked them both to please stay where they were.

She needed Blake to watch the Pines. And she hoped Jordan would be close by in the event that Hackett needed help. They both reluctantly accepted the roles she assigned them.

Her last call was to San Francisco to let Miles Diaz-Douglas know what was going on. Miles was chief operating office for Darcey's highly successful design firm. He was outraged when she told him he couldn't come to Alaska.

"What do you mean?" he demanded to know. "Am I a part of this team or not? And, girl, you know no man alive can stand up to me and my shotgun. Haven't I proved that?"

Darcey was careful not to let Miles hear her laughing softly as she recalled the night she and Trent were called to Miles' condo after the man responsible for the murder of Scott Douglas, Miles' husband, broke in. The would-be tough guy wound up unconscious with his face in his own urine after he wet his pants at the sight of Miles in his long, pink night shirt and pink fluffy slippers pointing a shotgun at him. Furious that the man had peed on his expensive rug, Miles used a heavy, iron skillet to render him unable to function.

She needed Miles to stay there and keep the company running. There was a lot to that job, she reminded him, especially since they now had an office in New Orleans.

"Well, maybe we need to open an office in Alaska, too," Miles said, somewhat mollified by her reference to his importance to the company.

When Robert returned, she told him about the conversations she'd had. She asked if he would check with his friend who was providing the airplane to see if he would accommodate a stop on the return flight to pick up passengers. A quick phone call earned an affirmative reply.

Ivy again was in charge of the kitchen as she prepared a jerk chicken. She had marinated the chicken for twenty four hours, in a variety of spices, including habanero peppers. Now it was in the oven.

After dinner, Betty planned to use the chicken carcass to make a broth and turn the whole thing into chicken soup before leaving for the airport the next morning. That would provide at least a couple of meals for Darcey and Robert.

It would also help to settle Darcey's mind. Betty's chicken soup was one of her daughter's favorite comfort foods from her childhood.

Darcey poured a nice Merlot for herself, Robert, and James. Betty and Ivy were sipping hot tea as they all sat again on the deck overlooking Cook Inlet. Kelli was having juice and feeling very grown up.

The railing around the deck was child proof. Made of heavy duty aluminum and iron, it featured shadows of moose and caribou and bears, much to Kelli's enjoyment. There were no more than four inches of space anywhere along the railing. Unlike glass, there was no chance of breakage and aesthetically it was far more pleasing to Kelli and the grownups alike than Plexiglas would have been.

"Did Trent ever tell you the story about the moose that got drunk and passed out on my back porch?" Robert asked.

"What?" Darcey laughed. "No, that's one drinking partner he's never mentioned."

"How would a moose get drunk?" Ivy asked. She had lived in New Orleans all her life. She didn't know much about moose.

"Trent takes bourbon to the horses when he's at the Pines," Betty said. "They like to smell it but they won't drink it."

"I doubt if a moose would drink it either," Robert said. "They like fermented fruit. You see, Darcey, I live just at the outskirts of town, on the side of Mount Juneau. I have a crabapple tree right at the edge of my back porch. I usually make jelly with the crabapples and I give a lot of them away. But that tree produces more than my neighbors and I can use. In the fall, the fruit ferments when it falls to the ground. Some of it ferments while it's still on the tree.

"It was October. Trent was a teenager. His dad took him out of school for a few days and brought him up for a hunting trip. We planned to go after Sitka black tail deer," Robert continued. "We had a fair amount of snow and it was cold enough to keep it from melting. Good hunting weather."

"Huh," Ivy said. "Sounds more like good fireplace weather to me."

"That, too," Robert agreed. "In fact, I was lighting a fire in the wood stove in my back room when I noticed we had a visitor. There was a cow moose curled up in the snow, sound asleep on my back porch. I warned Trent and his dad to be quiet when they came back to see our visitor.

"It was something," Robert said. "We don't see a lot of moose in Juneau. And that moose was drunk. Every now and then she would get up, stagger over to the crabapple tree, eat a little more of the fermented fruit, then drop back into the snow and fall asleep again.

"That went on for three days. I was scared to death that any minute we could have a drunk, 1,500-pound moose come crashing through the back door," Robert remembered. "By the third day I guess she'd had enough. We watched her stumble across the yard to the back fence. With those long legs she had no problem stepping over it. I always wondered if she had a hangover," he said.

"You're making that up," Ivy said. "Moose don't get drunk."

"This one did," Robert insisted. "Drunker than nine hundred dollars."

"What does that mean?" Betty asked. "Drunker than nine hundred dollars?"

"That means she was drunk. Really, really drunk."

The grownups all laughed at the image of the drunk moose. Kelli laughed, too, because everyone else was laughing. She pointed to the outline of the moose on the iron railing and said, "Moose."

"Yes, Kelli," Uncle Robert said. "Moose. And no crabapples."

Same Day. Dimension Unknown.

Trent wanted to leap out of bed and hold her. He knew she was there. He could sense her presence.

He couldn't open his eyes. He couldn't speak. He still didn't know if he was alive or dead. Or somewhere in between.

Darcey had been there. Now she was gone. He was alone again.

But he wasn't alone. Someone else was there. Someone he hadn't seen in a long time.

"Dad?" He couldn't open his eyes. He couldn't speak.

He saw his dad without opening his eyes.

He called out to him without speaking.

"Yes, son," he heard his dad say.

"But you're dead. You've been dead for a long time."

36

"Yes, son," he heard his dad say, "but I've never really left you."

"Am I dead? Does this mean I'm dead?"

"I don't know, son," was the answer he heard. "I don't think we will know that for a while yet."

"How can I see you and talk to you now?" Trent asked.

"I can't answer that, son," his dad replied. "I don't really understand it myself."

"This is just great," Trent said, venting his frustration. "I can't see or speak to my wife but here I am having a conversation with the image of my father who's been dead for more than twenty years."

Trent could feel his heart pounding in his chest. He heard the beeping from one of the machines to which he was attached speeding up. Suddenly the door opened and a nurse came in, alarmed by the increase of his heart rate. His father disappeared.

He tried to relax. The beeping sound slowed. The nurse was apparently satisfied that nothing untoward was happening. She left him alone.

Alone with his father who reappeared as the nurse left.

"Why did you leave when the nurse came in?"

"I don't know," was the reply. "That's just the way it is."

"Well, you were always good at leaving," Trent said, feeling the old burning bubble of anger swelling his chest. "You left my mother. You left me when I was too young to know why. I only knew you were gone and I missed you. I was afraid you would never come back."

"Yes, that's all true," his dad said, sadly. "We talked about all this years ago. I thought we had worked through it."

"I don't think the pain ever goes away completely," Trent said. "That feeling of abandonment is a forever kind of thing."

"I know, son, and I'm sorry. Leaving you and your mother was the worst mistake I ever made. It wasn't good between us but I could have tried harder. I should at least have loved you enough to stay."

"It's too bad she can't hear you say that." Trent spat the words bitterly.

His dad said nothing in response to that. He was silent for a moment.

"I never abandoned you completely, you know. We still spent a lot of time together. And I always tried to be there for you when you needed my help."

"That's not the same as being there every night and every weekend," Trent said. "You were sort of a quasi-father. And it doesn't make up for all the nights I heard my mother crying in her room."

"Yes, I know. She was a good woman. She deserved better."

"Yes, she sure did."

"But I was there for you when she passed away," his dad said. "When you lived with me in Baton Rouge I was there with you every night. And we had some great times. Remember our trips to Alaska? Remember the drunk moose on Robert's back porch?"

Trent laughed.

"Yeah, those were great years, Dad," he said. "But I always felt bad that Mom wasn't there to share them with us. I always felt like she got cheated."

"She did get cheated. I'm not denying that," his dad said. "And now you have a beautiful child. Your mom would be so proud that you named Kelli for her. And if I'd been given the chance to pick my son's wife, I would have picked Darcey."

"They're both great, aren't they?" Trent said. "I'm very lucky."

"And you're a great husband and father, son. I'm very proud of you."

"And now I might be abandoning them just as I was abandoned."

"No, it's not the same thing, son," his dad was quick to disagree. "I made a mistake. You did nothing wrong."

"I'm not even sure what happened," Trent said. "All I know is I'm probably dying and there's nothing I can do about it."

"That remains to be seen, son," his dad said. "We don't know yet."

The image of his dad faded away as the nurse returned. She checked all the machines attached to his unmoving body. She seemed satisfied.

He lay still. Unable to open his eyes. Unable to speak.

Was he alive? Was he dead? Was he somewhere in between?

Dimension still unknown.

38

July 11th

Jim Segal scanned the newspaper as he sipped the morning's first cup of coffee. Nothing. Not a mention of Trent Marshall.

He was certain it was a good kill. He saw the blood on Trent's head where the bullet struck. He watched him fall limply to the deck. Why hadn't there been some report in the news?

He was increasingly concerned that something had gone awry.

Suddenly exploding, he tossed the newspaper across the room, narrowly missing an expensive lamp.

Calm down, he told himself. It wouldn't help to lose his self control. He could do nothing until he had more information.

He briefly considered sending McGraw to the hospital in Juneau but rejected the idea. It wouldn't be smart to appear interested in the shooting. That would show a connection to the victim. A connection he didn't need.

If Marshall wasn't dead, he might have been flown to Anchorage. There were specialists in brain injuries in Anchorage. If he was still alive, he was probably in one of the city's hospitals.

There were three main hospitals in Anchorage. There was also a specialty hospital where patients were sent when no more could be done for them elsewhere. If Marshall was still alive his injury would be so serious as to get him sent to the specialists there.

He thought about sending Jayne to see what she could find out. But she couldn't just go wandering through the halls looking into rooms. Someone would start asking questions. And if she found him, then what? With her perverse addiction to murder, anything could happen if someone got in her way.

He didn't need anyone asking questions. And he sure didn't need Jayne wandering through the hospital, armed and thirsty for blood. He went to his bedroom to shower, shave, and get dressed for the day.

It was sixty-nine degrees with not a cloud to be seen as the Gulfstream prepared to take off. A pleasant, short sleeve shirt day in Anchorage.

Kelli was squirming in her seat. Betty strapped the three year old in, then placed herself in the seat next to her. She looked around at the aircraft's luxurious cabin.

"My, my, this is some airplane," she remarked.

"I thought flying first class and that boat we were on were something," Ivy replied. "But this airplane… this really is something. Really something."

APD Chief Kline had sent two unmarked cars to transport the small group to the airport. True to his word, none of the officers asked any questions of Hackett. They did their best to avoid attracting attention. Fortunately, the Gulfstream was parked well away from the main terminals so the departing group attracted little attention.

So they thought.

Segal's phone rang as he was shaving. He recognized the number. He answered but said nothing. He listened.

They were getting the family out of Alaska. But Darcey Anderson was staying. What did that mean? Was Marshall still alive? Apparently, but perhaps not for long.

Segal was already considering the meaning of this new information and how he could use it. He didn't have a plan yet. There were too many unknowns.

He didn't know where this was going but it was smart to be prepared. He would talk to someone in New Orleans later in the day.

It was ninety degrees outside when the Gulfstream's wheels were lowered for landing at Louis Armstrong International Airport. The pilot taxied the aircraft away from the main terminal to a private hangar where two unmarked vehicles waited.

Hackett went down the stairs first. He wanted to be certain that his charges would be safe when they exited the airplane.

A man who was about the same age as Trent stepped forward.

"Mr. Hackett?" he asked.

"Yes, that's me," Hackett replied, looking around with expert, searching eyes.

"I'm Jordan Baron. Darcey asked me to meet y'all and see you safely to their home."

"Glad to see you, Captain Baron," Hackett responded. "Darcey speaks very highly of you."

Forty-five minutes later, having wound their way through the crowded highways and streets of New Orleans, the two vehicles pulled up in front of the long brick wall on Governor Nicholls Street near Royal, which blocked the street view of Trent and Darcey's home. Baron worked the code that opened the larger of two faded green gates, allowing the vehicles to drive into the courtyard.

It was a beautiful residence, Hackett thought. No doubt about that. He was more interested in determining a defensive plan. He saw immediately why Darcey described the home as a fortress. It would be difficult for anyone to get in. If they got in, the home could be effectively defended. It would be next to impossible for any intruders to abscond with their lives intact.

It was agreed that they should avoid attracting unnecessary attention. Baron would stop by from time to time but that wouldn't be unusual. As a family friend he was often there. He would have an unmarked car drive by a few times a day. Hackett also put Baron's phone number into his phone so he could call quickly if he needed to.

Hackett suggested that Ivy move from her apartment into the main house.

"Ain't nobody going to chase me out of my home," she said.

"How about if I just ask you to please join us?" Hackett said, wisely taking a diplomatic approach with the stubborn woman. "If anyone succeeded in getting inside that wall, you being in a separate building would make their job easier and mine harder. It's like the four of us running into a bear in the woods. If we all keep calm and move close to each other, we'll look to the bear like an animal bigger than him and he'll head in the other direction."

"Now that makes sense," Ivy said. "Just let me get a few things."

"I never heard that about defending against a bear. Does it really work?" Baron asked.

"That's what they say," Hackett replied with an unrestrained look of delight. "Personally, I would rather have a really big gun."

Hackett's gun came out when he was alone. Darcey had told him that Baron would give him plenty of leeway regarding weapons but there was no point in putting the officer in an uncomfortable position.

Stepping out onto the gallery outside his assigned bedroom, Hackett looked over the grounds. From the second floor he could just see over the wall. It was a good defensive position. He began to work quickly and efficiently, moving a chair and table into place.

He drew the strange looking revolver from the holster on his belt. The German arms maker Korth produced some of the finest weapons available anywhere, and the most expensive. The nine-millimeter revolver, called the Korth Sky Marshal, was an effective weapon. As Korth weapons went, it was also relatively cheap at $1,000.

With its blunt nose, it looked like it had no barrel at all. The cylinder, holding six rounds, swung out for reloading. To assist in rapid reloading, the Sky Marshal had small, spring-loaded extractor tabs at the base of the cartridge case. The tabs force spent cartridges out of the chambers when the ejector rod is pushed. Weighing less than twenty ounces, the small weapon had sufficient power for Hackett's needs.

The defensive position he prepared allowed him to rest his arm on the gallery's railing to steady any shots. He was satisfied.

Having finished his preparations, he returned to the first floor. There he found Ivy and Betty preparing a grocery list for Baron while the cop crawled around on the floor with Kelli riding him like a horse.

"Gittie up, horsie," the child said through her giggles. Clearly the policeman was a favorite playmate for the little girl when the family was in New Orleans.

He and Baron agreed that for the time being the family should remain behind the brick wall. Hence, the police captain volunteered to make the grocery run. He would arrange for future deliveries directly by the grocer.

He also promised to bring an assortment of po' boys and fries. There would be oysters, shrimp, fried catfish, and roast beef "debris" sandwiches. Kelli would get a fried shrimp po' boy which she would promptly deconstruct and eat the shrimp one by one with her fingers.

Hackett wandered into the room that Trent used for an office and library. His attention was drawn to the glass display case placed in the center of the rear wall. An admirer of fine weapons himself, he marveled at the contents.

The 1862 Colt alone would attract attention. But he was mesmerized by the matched pair of original Deringers, a beautiful set of the small, single shot pistols. And the LeMat. Monk told Hackett that Trent had brought a reproduction of the handgun on his trip to Alaska. But this was an original model probably produced sometime around 1860.

On a small, slightly elevated shelf, lay a gold coin. Hackett didn't know its significance. But it added to the mystery of the display of rare weapons.

It was a mildly cool evening in Anchorage. At five o'clock, Monk mixed martinis for them. He and Darcey again sat on the deck, sipping their cocktails.

The crew of the Gulfstream would overnight in New Orleans and return the next day after making a stop in San Francisco to pick up Christopher Booth and Nancy Patrick. They would arrive in the early afternoon, Anchorage time.

This evening they would have Betty's chicken soup for dinner. Darcey had put two heads of garlic in the oven to roast. They would smear it on slices of crusty bread to eat with the soup.

After Darcey's family was in the air and on the way to the safety of the New Orleans house, Monk went with her to the hospital. Dr. Shannon told them there was no change in Trent's condition.

Darcey asked if the swelling in his brain had gone down. Dr. Shannon repeated that there was no change.

"But you said three days…" Darcey protested.

"I said 'usually' three days," Dr. Shannon corrected. "It's not precise."

After dinner Darcey would go back to the hospital to visit with Trent for a while before going to bed. She would like to stay there with him but knew that wasn't a good idea.

He needed her to do what she was doing. She needed to be working with Robert, Christopher, and Nancy to find out who was behind the shooting and bring whoever it was down. To do that she needed to get sufficient sleep. You can't find that in a hospital hallway.

It was late in Louisiana when Segal talked to his New Orleans contact. The report was concise. The caller had observed the New Orleans house and described its excellent strategic position. It would be difficult to get to the family in that house if Segal wanted to do so. If it came to that, he'd have to find a way to flush them out. At this point, he preferred to leave them alone.

Segal wasn't an impetuous decision maker. He needed time to think. He also was beginning to think this affair had the potential to rapidly move in an uncontrollable direction. He couldn't afford to let that happen.

In Southeast Alaska, Captain Place was on the bridge in the dusk of the northern summer night. They were in Alaska waters just south of Ketchikan. Dancer would cruise leisurely through the waters northwest of Ketchikan for the next four days. His wealthy guests would spend the time fishing and enjoying the scenery. Of course, they weren't guests at all and certainly weren't wealthy. They were hired to play their roles. Their job was to wave and smile at any passing vessels. Not a bad job, Place thought.

He would leisurely circle Prince of Wales Island before pointing his bow south. The course would be set for a small, secluded cove on Dall Island, one of several identified by Segal and McGraw as sites for Dancer and its companion vessels to meet their Asian partners to transfer cargo. There were only about twenty people living on Dall Island. The transfer of cargo should be unobserved.

Place was on schedule to be in the cove, ready for the transfer, by the night of July 15th.

July 12th

Darcey stepped out onto the deck, coffee in hand. Only a few fluffy, white clouds sailed through the blue northern sky. The weather forecast called for temperatures in the seventies. Very warm by Alaska standards.

She was learning that there was a good ten-degree psychological difference in weather between Alaska and the Continental U.S. In San Francisco or New Orleans, a day in the seventies would be pleasant. In Alaska, it felt unquestionably warm.

She was coming to love the view from the deck. Looking to the north, she could see Denali, at 20,320 feet the highest peak in North America, sparkling white. Known until recently as Mount McKinley, a presidential executive order had changed it back to the name Alaskans always called it. She understood now, she thought, why Trent had such fond memories of his trips north with his father.

Her heart began to race as her phone rang. It was Dr. Shannon. She closed her eyes for a moment before answering. She prayed it was good news.

"The swelling in Trent's brain has gone down," Dr. Shannon said. "I thought you'd like to know that. Today I'm going to replace the small piece of his skull that I removed earlier."

The relief was overwhelming. For a moment, she thought she might pass out from the rush that flowed through her.

"Thank you for calling, Dr. Shannon," she finally responded. "I'll be right there."

Monk had just poured himself a cup of coffee and was coming to join her on the deck as she suddenly dashed past him, almost knocking him down.

45

"The swelling in his brain has reduced!" she shouted. "They're going to put his head back together this morning! I don't have time to wait for you, Robert."

"Go, Darcey," he called after her. "Don't worry about me. Let me know how it's going when you can."

After Darcey left, Monk sat on the deck sipping coffee and thinking. He was being a cop again. Doing what he enjoyed most about being a cop. Working on a puzzle.

From the beginning of his career he understood that the cases assigned to him were nothing more than puzzles. Puzzles often involving bad things happening to good people. Puzzles nonetheless.

The puzzle in front of him now had very few visible pieces. Someone, unknown, tried to assassinate Trent Marshall. So far the attempt wasn't successful.

At the same time *Nanuq*'s deck hand was killed, presumably by the same person who shot Trent. Why was the deck hand killed? It wasn't necessary. It was even risky. There had to be a good reason.

He went back inside to refill his coffee cup, then walked across the room to the library and office in which sat the desk where both he and Darcey had set their laptops to connect to the condo's Internet. He looked in a drawer to find an old-fashioned pad of paper and a pen.

Pulling his phone from his pocket, he dialed Captain Hannigan's number. He didn't know where the *Nanuq* was. He hoped it was within range of a mobile tower.

Hannigan answered after the third ring. He was still docked in Auke Bay. The local police and the State Troopers' Bureau of Investigation had held him in port for the past few days as they launched their investigation. An investigation that so far had gone nowhere.

Monk gave the captain a report on Trent's condition, including what was going on today. Hannigan said he was hopeful all went well.

Monk asked him what he knew about his late deck hand.

"Not much really," Hannigan answered. "His name was Warren Perkins. He was from Seattle. At least that's where he lived. I don't know where he was from originally. We don't even know who to contact or what to do with his body. The Maritime Union is trying to find his family."

46

"Did he have any friends in Seattle? Did you ever see him with anyone?"

"No. When we were in port he spent most evenings in a bar nearby. A hangout for longshoremen and seamen. I think he got drunk most every night but he always showed up sober and on time for work so I had no complaint with how he spent his nights."

"Do you remember the name of the bar?" Monk asked.

"Let me think. Some kind of Greek name. Cad something. Cadious? Caduceous? Yeah, that's it. Caduceous."

"The symbol of the messenger of the gods. Fancy."

"Far from it," Hannigan scoffed. "It's a dive bar trying to sound classy. It's the kind of place where you would have got yourself shanghaied a century ago. Could still happen, I'd bet."

"You don't happen to have a picture of him, do you?"

"Yes, as a matter of fact I do. You can see it online if you go to our website. We posted pictures of our entire crew. Warren is on the far right. He has a round face with a receding hairline and always seemed to have a three-day growth of beard on his face," Hannigan said. "If it would help, I can send you just that picture."

Monk asked him to send it via text to his phone. After he ended the call, he looked at what he had written on the pad of paper.

Warren Perkins.

Caduceous.

Seattle.

Someone had to go to Seattle. Or they had to find a contact there who would do some leg work for them.

Then he wrote two more names.

Jim Segal?

Cameron McGraw?

Both question marks.

Both on his list strictly on the basis of an old cop's gut instinct. Nothing more than that. Instinct.

It was almost noon before Dr. Shannon appeared in the family waiting room. Darcey had become increasingly concerned as the hours ticked by. The look on the doctor's face, however, was reassuring.

47

"No problems," Dr. Shannon said with a pleased twinkle in her eyes. "The surgery went well. Trent has been put back together and is doing fine."

Darcey let out the breath she had unknowingly been holding since the doctor walked into the room.

"Thank you so much, Doctor," she said. "When can I see him?"

"You can look through the window again now if you wish. He's in intensive care. If he continues doing well, we'll move him out of ICU into a room by tomorrow morning. At that point you can be with him."

"Just try to hold me back," Darcey said, excitedly. "What happens now?"

"He needs more time to heal," was the answer. "We'll keep him in an induced coma for probably a week or so. Then we'll slowly bring him out of it. We'll have to observe his reactions every step of the way. It won't do him any good to rush the process."

"Any guess on when he might be discharged from the hospital?"

"Well, that's hard to say. If he responds positively when he comes out of the coma, maybe we can let you have him in another couple of weeks," the doctor said. "There's no set rule. From now on it's really up to him. We just have to take it a day at a time. And after he leaves here I wouldn't plan on him traveling for another month."

Darcey was adding up the weeks in her head. She was going to have to make more living arrangements. And how could she be parted from Kelli for that long?

As the doctor said, one day at a time. Today she had to focus on finding the shooter.

"Wow!" Nancy Patrick said as she stood on the deck looking at the Sleeping Lady and a hundred miles beyond to Denali. "This place is fantastic even by your standards, Darcey."

Nancy and her companion, San Francisco Police Homicide Captain Christopher Booth, had become accustomed to the lifestyle of their wealthy friends. In the beginning of their friendship Nancy felt some resentment. On the salaries of two cops they couldn't afford anything close to the homes that Trent and Darcey owned in San Francisco and New Orleans. But that quickly passed. She learned to enjoy the importance of having good friends. Especially friends you could count on to have your back when bad guys came at you with guns. Even better if they were rich.

Darcey was surprised at Nancy's comment when she introduced her friend to Robert.

"That's former Detective Sergeant Patrick," Nancy said.

"Former?" Darcey said. "I'm not prescient so you have to tell me what happened that I don't know."

"I quit," Nancy said.

Darcey was stunned.

"You quit your job? Why?"

"Christopher asked his boss for two weeks off to come up here and got approval with no questions," Nancy explained. "My boss refused. So I quit."

"When I asked for your help, Nancy, I didn't mean for it to cost you your job!"

"I was thinking about quitting anyway," Nancy said. "After Operation Den of Snakes was successful in bringing down Rossi's criminal federation, I was led to believe a promotion was coming my way. But it never happened. The Rooster kept losing the paperwork or something. So when he said no to my leave request, I quit."

The Rooster was the name the officers at his precinct in Richmond, just outside of San Francisco, called her boss, or former boss, Captain Terry Wooster, behind his back.

Christopher's career moved upward quickly after the successful operation the four of them had worked on together in cooperation with the FBI San Francisco office. His captain, Fess Albright, retired. With the arrest and indictment of Deputy Chief Amanda Justice, there was a shakeup in the chief's office. Lieutenant Billy Mitchum, who should have been in line for Albright's job was transferred instead to SFPD headquarters. Booth was tapped to jump a grade and take the captain's chair.

He felt guilty that he had moved up and Nancy had not. But she wouldn't stand for that. It wasn't his fault that her boss was a jerk. Every cop in the Bay area knew him. None respected him. As long as he was between her and the Richmond PD chief, Nancy's career was going nowhere.

Nancy and Christopher both were wearing jackets, thinking it would be colder than they were used to. When they discovered it was a relatively warm day, they stripped off their jackets. In doing so, both revealed that they were armed.

"A Glock 20, right?" Monk asked Christopher. "I carried one of those for several years when I was with the State Troopers. It was their sidearm of choice."

"It packs a lot of punch," Christopher said. "Powerful enough to use for hunting fair sized game."

Robert was especially drawn to the nickel-plated revolver with wood grips on Nancy's hip.

"Is that a Smith & Wesson Model 19 or Model 66?" he asked. "Has to be one or the other."

"Model 19," Nancy said. "It belonged to my dad. He was a cop, too."

The Model 19 was the first handgun built to handle a magnum cartridge. Nancy's weapon had a four inch barrel. The cylinder held six .357 magnum cartridges. Also a lot of punch for a handgun. The Model 66 was a later version of the same weapon.

"With my hideaway Glock, Trent's reproduction LeMat, and the single shot .410 handgun that Darcey's packing we're in good shape for a close in gunfight," Monk observed.

Booth looked around.

"But this shooter works at long range," he reminded them. "Aren't we pushing our luck out here in the open?"

"I think we're ok," Monk said. "We're pretty high up in the air here. On this side of the building he would have to fire up at about a fifty degree angle. That would be a difficult shot. It could be made but the shooter would have to know the algorithm necessary to accurately judge the shot. And he would have to be in the open.

"To reduce the degree of angle and give himself cover, he would have to be on a boat or on the other side of the inlet. If he tries from a boat he would still be in the open. The boat's movement would make the shot difficult if not impossible. And the other side of the inlet is out of range even for this guy. I think we're safe here, especially with these iron animals that child-proofed the deck to make it safe for Kelli."

"Nobody at the airport gave you any trouble about being armed, Nancy?" Darcey asked.

"Nope. I said I quit. I didn't say I turned in my badge and gun. I just walked out. And since we were boarding a private jet at a private hangar, nobody was looking anyway."

Darcey laughed. Monk decided he liked these two cops.

Darcey had already reported to Christopher and Nancy on today's news regarding Trent. For the next hour and a half Robert briefed them on what little information they had so far. They discussed Robert's view that this puzzle would lead them well beyond the attempted assassination of Trent Marshall. They listened to his theory that they were faced with a complicated conspiracy extending from Anchorage to Juneau and Southeast Alaska to Seattle and perhaps farther.

He showed them the picture of Warren Perkins, told them about Caduceous, the bar that Perkins hung out in when he was in port, and noted that someone had to go to Seattle unless they could come up with a contact there to check out the bar.

He asked them if the names Jim Segal and Cameron McGraw meant anything to them. They did not.

"But I've got a good relationship with the FBI Agent in Charge in San Francisco. He might be able to help us with them," Booth said.

At 4:30 Darcey called a halt to the discussion.

"Y'all know five o'clock is cocktail hour at our house," Darcey reminded them. "I suggest we take a break now. You two can freshen up and get settled in your bedroom. Then we'll gather on the deck for peach martinis."

There was a bit of melancholy in the smiles. Christopher and Nancy knew that peach martinis were one of Trent's specialties. They had been served at their wedding at the Pines. Trent had made them for the group in San Francisco many times.

"But for dinner I suggest we go out," she continued. "With all the activity today, I haven't had time to even think about cooking. The hottest place in town is JS Bistro. I took the liberty of making reservations for us this evening if that's ok with y'all. And just *coincidentally*," she added, emphasis on the word *coincidentally*, "JS Bistro is owned by Jim Segal."

"Interesting selection," Robert said, an amused look on his face. "I've always said there's no such thing as coincidence in crime, corruption, or politics."

They all had heard Trent express the same view.

Now they knew that he learned it from Robert Monk.

Seated at their table in JS Bistro, Darcey asked their waiter to bring them two orders of albondigas as appetizers. The small Spanish meatballs arrived tasting of garlic and spicy chorizo sausage with a hint of nutmeg. They were accompanied by a tomato sauce for dipping.

While Darcey and her guests sipped their cocktails, nibbled at the albondigas, and studied the menu, Segal entered the restaurant. He had been there earlier in the day but had gone home to check in with McGraw and Captain Place. Satisfied that all was going well in Southeast, Segal returned to his restaurant to play host to the dinner crowd.

It was Segal's favorite part of his day. He played his role of host at a fine dining restaurant to its limit. He even dressed the part, appearing each evening in black tie, aberrant wear for a city known for casual clothing.

Stopping at the Maitre D's station, he looked at the list of reservations. Surprisingly he discovered Darcey Anderson's name on the list. On most nights he would move from table to table greeting his guests. Seeing her reservation for a party of four made him sense danger. He walked quickly to the end of the bar and up the stairs, attempting to keep his face averted without appearing unusually strained.

Jayne Colombo, as usual was at her desk when he entered.

"What's wrong with you?" she asked.

"Nothing. Nothing's wrong with me. Why do you ask?"

"You just look a little shook up is all," she said. "Not your usual confident, bon vivant style."

"Trent Marshall's wife is here with three friends," he said. "That seems a little unusual to me."

"Oh, relax. They wanted to have dinner. This is a very well known and popular restaurant. You're making something out of nothing."

Segal was trying to decide if Darcey Anderson showing up in his restaurant was significant. Was it something that should concern him? He thought perhaps not. He hoped not. The last thing he wanted was more people dying. That would attract too much attention. The sort of attention he wanted to avoid at all cost.

"Yeah, you're right," he said. "Everybody has to eat."

From her station in the kitchen, the young woman with the red and black striped hair watched Segal walk quickly through the restaurant. Weird, she thought. He usually made a point to greet everyone in the building when he came in. Something must be up.

Christopher Booth watched Segal walk the length of the bar. When the restaurateur disappeared upstairs, Booth told his companions to continue studying their menus.

"Don't look up or turn around," he cautioned. "We might have a picture to put on one of our puzzle pieces."

"See somebody you recognize?" Monk questioned.

"Sure did."

"Save it for later. Restaurants are the worst places to talk business," the old cop said. "You never know who is listening."

"Whatever else he might be up to, Jim Segal puts a good meal on the table," Darcey said.

They were in the sitting room at the condo, looking out to the east over the lights of the city framed in the shadow box of the Chugach Mountains. While Monk thought they were safe on the west deck, he was not as confident about the east side. There were too many tall buildings the shooter might use for cover and the less severe angle of fire would make it an easier shot.

"So who is he?" Robert asked. "Someone you know?"

"Oh yes," Christopher said. "Before he was Jim Segal, he was Pietro Greco, aka Peter Greco. Don Rossi's consigliere and underboss. I always thought he was the real brain behind the Rossi Mafia family."

"That explains what's going on," Darcey said. "Segal, or Greco, is taking revenge for the destruction of the alliance in San Francisco."

"I don't think it's as simple as that," Christopher replied. "I've wondered what happened to Greco after his boss was murdered. Without Rossi in charge, the leaders of the three other organizations that made up the alliance were all murdered in rapid succession.

"All four were known to keep large sums of emergency cash in their homes. When we got to each of them, their safes had been opened and were empty. In addition, Rossi's safe deposit box at his bank, in which he was thought to keep a couple of million, was empty. Only Rossi and Greco were authorized access. Not even Rossi's wife could get into it but by that time she was back east with her family.

"Finally, one of the gang leaders had indulged in a very expensive yacht. Cost seven or eight million. It disappeared about the same time as Greco and the money."

"Doesn't sound like simple revenge to me," Robert chimed in.

"I think Greco saw Trent and feared he would be recognized," Christopher said.

"And that makes me think my theory that we're onto a large and complicated conspiracy is correct," Robert said. "If it was only fear of being recognized Segal, or Greco, could have just stayed out of sight. A lot less risky than assassinating a well-known man in broad daylight."

Darcey called Kelli every morning and again in the evening before the little girl was put to bed. She visited Trent each evening before she retired for the night herself.

Nancy went with her this evening. Dr. Shannon told Darcey earlier in the day that, if no complications developed overnight, Trent would be moved out of ICU into a regular room. At least what passed as a regular room at this hospital, which was designed to care for patients whose chances for survival were questionable. Each of the regular rooms was packed with esoteric medical technology. Darcey didn't know what all the machines did. She only cared that they were keeping Trent alive.

The two women stood outside the ICU looking in at Trent. His head was now wrapped in a white bandage. He was unmoving. He looked lifeless but he was breathing with the assistance of one of the machines.

Neither spoke. There was nothing to say.

Jayne Colombo's car was parked in a far, darkened corner of the cheap hotel's lot. She sat behind the wheel. Her face flushed. Her breath came in gasps. Her eyes were closed in sweet memory. She was lost in whatever it was that served as excitement for a psychopath.

In one of the hotel's rooms a woman lay in a bed. She had no breath at all. Her face wasn't flushed but was graying as lividity began its slow work drawing blood from a non-beating heart to the lowest points of the woman's body. The three holes stitching her torso bled some but had already lost the drainage struggle to gravity. The woman felt nothing. Her eyes were open. Staring at the ceiling. Seeing darkness. Only darkness.

Colombo struggled to gain control of herself. She started the engine. She had to get out of here before someone noticed. It wouldn't do for Segal to discover she had returned to satisfying her perverted addiction.

She knew he would be furious with her. He had not sent her out on a kill since she arrived. She knew his priority was to attract no negative attention. She was surprised when he made the hit on Marshall himself.

She tried. She really tried. A year went by. She could stand it no longer. Her need had to be satisfied.

She let a man pick her up in a bar. It was good. Not as good as it would have been if she could have described it to Segal. But it satisfied her.

For six months.

Then she found another man.

Another six months and then tonight. This time a woman. The sex of her victim didn't matter to her. Man or woman. Either satisfied her peculiar need. The perverse need to kill. She didn't understand it. It was, even to her, inexplicable.

She didn't care. She didn't think about it. She only knew that she would again have to satisfy her need.

She drove slowly to the apartment she rented in midtown Anchorage. She didn't want to live too close to Segal's home downtown. She knew there would be more times when she would move quietly through the night seeking relief. She didn't want him to see that.

Later, as she lay in bed, she caressed the machine pistol that released her passion as it relieved her unlucky companions of life.

For the first time in weeks she slept through the night.

July 13th

It was going to be another warm, sunny day in Anchorage. Darcey awoke early only to find Robert already up and dressed. He had made coffee. She gratefully accepted a cup.

"Robert, there are some fresh cobs of corn in the refrigerator," she said. "Would you mind shucking three of them and cutting the kernels off while I call Kelli?"

"Will do," was the quick reply.

She took her cup back to her bedroom. She felt this stone in her belly as she thought of the separation that she knew would continue for longer than she would like. She hated being apart from her daughter but she couldn't yet leave. As Dr. Shannon continually told her, one day at a time.

After the call, she showered and dressed quickly. In the kitchen, she whipped up a batter for corn fritters. She beat an egg white until it was stiff, then gently folded it into the batter which already featured the corn kernels Robert had cut from the cobs, green onion, minced ham, and a little thyme to add savory to the sweet.

Nancy came in while she was mixing the batter.

"Looks good. What is it?" the former detective asked. Nancy was not accomplished in the kitchen but had been learning since becoming friends with Darcey and Trent.

"Corn fritters for breakfast," Darcey said. "While I'm making the fritters would you put a dipping sauce together?"

"Sure. Just tell me how."

While Darcey dropped the batter by the spoonful into hot oil, Nancy prepared the dipping sauce by melting a stick of butter. At Darcey's instruction, she added maple syrup and several generous dashes of Tabasco.

56

By the time Christopher showed up, the table was set with a mound of tempting fritters and a small bowl of dipping sauce by each plate.

"What's our plan for today?" Nancy asked, as she spooned a little of the sweet and spicy sauce over the two fritters on her plate.

"I would like you to come with me again to the hospital, if you don't mind," Darcey said. "If Trent made it through the night with no complications, they're moving him out of ICU this morning. It'll be the first time I've been allowed in the room with him since we got to Anchorage."

"I'll be right beside you," Nancy promised.

"Christopher, the chief of police here is a friend of mine and is committed to working with us," Robert said. "In return I want to keep him informed on any new leads we turn up. I'd like you to go with me to his office this morning to brief him on what you know about our Jim Segal."

"Glad to."

"Then I think it's time for you to call your FBI buddy in San Francisco," Robert continued. "I remain convinced there's far more at stake here than Segal's fear of being recognized. I'm curious to know if the feds have noticed any uptick on criminal activity of any kind on the west coast."

A few blocks away, Segal sat in his condo with the morning's second cup of coffee. He didn't often eat breakfast. He was moderate when it came to meals. He considered overindulgence in food as harmful as tobacco, alcohol or drugs.

He hadn't heard from his contact in New Orleans the day before. He assumed that meant there was nothing to report. Marshall's family remained forted up behind their brick wall.

He was still troubled by Darcey Anderson showing up in his restaurant last night with three others. He wanted to believe Jayne was right. It probably meant nothing other than four people going out to dinner at one of the city's most popular restaurants.

What bothered him was her three companions. One of them could be the old man who joined them on the *Nanuq* just before the hit. If Marshall was alive and had been flown to Anchorage the old man might have accompanied the family. That wouldn't be out of the ordinary. It would be alarming but not unusual.

But who could the other two be? Others who might recognize him, he wondered?

At best, it was a complication. He didn't like complications. And that much complication would be deadly.

Darcey was disappointed to find Trent still in ICU. Dr. Shannon was with him. She came out to meet Darcey.

"I don't think he's ready to be moved yet," the doctor said. "Maybe by this afternoon. Maybe tomorrow."

Darcey thought she might faint. She felt Nancy take her hand. The doctor was talking but Darcey didn't hear what she was saying. Her world was spinning out of control.

Dr. Shannon realized Darcey was on the verge of fainting. She helped her into a chair and asked Nancy to find some water. The doctor herself held Darcey's hands.

"Trent isn't responding as quickly as we had hoped, Darcey," Dr. Shannon spoke quietly. "But it doesn't mean he's losing the fight. We can't rush his recovery. That would be the worst thing we could do for him."

Darcey nodded, wordlessly, as she sipped the water Nancy brought her.

"It's equally important now for you to remain strong," Dr. Shannon continued. "That's the best thing you can do for Trent now. Strength and patience."

After Dr. Shannon left, the two women stood at the window looking in at Trent. His head was now wrapped in a white bandage. He was breathing with the assistance of a machine. But he was breathing.

"Your husband is one tough guy, Darcey," Nancy said. "He got shot in the head and he looks like he's only having a nice nap. Remember, too, when the dirty cop slipped that nasty bug into Trent's clothes. The bug's bite put a virus in his blood that doctors had never seen before. He survived that. Does he still have symptoms from that?"

"Not many in the last couple of years. The antidote and vaccine Dr. Raymond made from the powder Preston Johnson gave us before he died seems to have worked."

Johnson was Darcey's friend and neighbor in San Francisco. Darcey didn't know he was also a legendary assassin known as Jimmy Shadow who did his job in ways that made it difficult to know how his victims died. He had supplied the bug to former New Orleans cop Steve Burgess who sought revenge against Marshall.

When Johnson discovered that Burgess used the bug in an attempt to kill his friend Trent, he lured Burgess to his home. There it was Burgess who died, run through with the steel blade concealed in the cane Johnson was never without. Before he died after drinking a rare champagne to which he had added poison to his own glass, the old man gave Trent a powder from which the cure could be made.

"And then there were the lunatics who tried to kill you and Trent and your mother in Louisiana because they thought a fortune in stolen Confederate gold was stashed on your family's farm," Nancy reminded her friend.

"Yeah, another crooked cop and my crazy, long lost distant cousin from Colorado. Well, they were right," Darcey said. "The gold was there though we never knew it until Trent figured it out. And if it weren't for those lunatics we would never have met. I wouldn't have Trent and Kelli now."

"But there are less stressful ways to meet men."

"Yeah, and I'm getting tired of people trying to kill my husband," Darcey declared.

"I think you guys need to get a new hobby. Take up bowling or something."

"Life with Trent Marshall is never dull," Darcey said with a sad smile as she continued to stare at her wounded husband. "That won't change, Nancy. Ever."

At ten o'clock Robert introduced SFPD Captain Christopher Booth to APD Chief Ben Kline. They talked cop stuff briefly and soon were on a first name basis.

Robert told the chief they had a new development.

"I didn't want to discuss it on the phone, Ben," Robert said. "I brought Christopher along because he's the one who made the connection."

"I recognized one of your leading citizens last night, Ben," Booth said, "as a very dangerous criminal who disappeared from the Bay area four years ago. Jim Segal, who I understand owns JS Bistro, is really Pietro Greco, or sometimes Peter Greco."

The chief was taken completely by surprise.

"Jim Segal?" Kline said. "That's hard to believe."

"What do you really know about Jim Segal, aka Peter Greco, aka Pietro Greco?" Robert asked.

"Not much really," the chief replied. "He hasn't been here long. He's a native Alaskan who made it good elsewhere and came home with a ton of money. Or at least that's the story I heard. Never had any reason to doubt it until now. What I do know is that on any given night his restaurant is filled with some of the most important people in the state. So what do you know about him?"

The last statement was directed at Booth.

"Pietro Greco was both consigliere and underboss to Jonathan Rossi, the last don of the Rossi Mafia family in San Francisco," Christopher responded. "I always thought he was the real brains behind the family's business ventures.

"Whoever had the brains convinced three other criminal organizations to join the Rossi family in a super federation of crime. The Thai gang Spitting Cobra. Some outlaw bikers calling themselves the Barons of Lucifer. A mysterious Middle Eastern group known only as the Scourge. Together the four of them could put an army on the street."

Kline whistled.

"That's impressive," he said. "But what does it all have to do with Trent Marshall?

"I was assigned to figure out how the alliance was managing to do business, specifically how they were moving illegal money around the globe and getting it into the legitimate economy. Since I had no experience in such things, I figured somebody wanted to be sure any investigation into the gangs' businesses wouldn't go anywhere.

"Jordan Baron is a cop in New Orleans who I worked with on a case involving both our cities. He knew Trent had knowledge of international money laundering from a story he had published back in his days as an investigative reporter. Jordan got us together. With cooperation from the FBI and the police force in the suburban community where the Barons had their headquarters, we developed a strategy we called Operation Den of Snakes. The goal was to disrupt the trust among the four groups so they would turn on each other. The strategy worked."

"So our boy Segal escaped the net?" Kline asked.

"I think he did a little more than that," Booth replied. "The leaders of all four gangs were assassinated by someone. They all kept large sums of cash at their headquarters as emergency money. Each time we got to the scene of one of the murders, the money was gone. Additionally, Rossi was thought to keep a safe deposit box with another large amount of cash. As his underboss, Greco would have had access to that as well.

"Finally, a very expensive yacht owned by the leader of Spitting Cobra disappeared about the same time," Booth wound up his briefing.

"When did all this happen?" Kline asked.

"Four years ago."

"Hmmm. I think it was around that time that Segal showed up here. It was obvious he had a lot of money and didn't need to work. For a while, he just wandered around the state. He said he'd been gone for a long time and wanted to get reacquainted with his native land," Kline said. "He opened the restaurant about a year after he got here. Said he was bored, wanted something to do, and had always wanted to own a restaurant."

"Did he ever tell anyone how he made his fortune?" Monk asked.

"No, he was pretty vague about it. This is all quite a coincidence, isn't it?"

Monk shook his head.

"I know what you're thinking, Robert," Kline said, sounding more lighthearted than he felt. "There's no such thing as coincidence in crime, corruption or politics. So where do we go from here?"

"I thought Segal spotted Trent and feared he would be recognized if Trent saw him," Christopher said. "But Robert thinks there's more to it than that."

"If that's all it was, Segal could have just stayed out of sight until Trent and his family left town. It was obvious they wouldn't be around for long," Monk said. "No, I think there's something big going on that Segal wants to protect. He didn't want to take the chance that Trent might stumble onto something. Don't yet know what it is but I think it goes beyond Alaska."

"Do you have any more leads?" Kline asked.

"Just one possible," Robert said. "You know the shooter also killed Warren Perkins, the *Nanuq*'s deck hand. I've been asking myself why he would do that. It seems unnecessarily risky unless there was a good reason. The *Nanuq*'s owner told me that Perkins spent every evening at a waterfront dive bar in Seattle when they were in their home port. I wonder if Segal somehow found out that Trent and his family were planning a private Alaska cruise. If so, I can theorize that he might have flown to Seattle himself. He could easily arrange to meet the deck hand at his favorite bar. He could probably just as easily bribe Perkins. With a member of the crew on his payroll, Segal would know where Trent was on any given day.

"We're thinking about one of us flying to Seattle to talk to people at the bar Perkins hung out in. If we show them a picture of Segal we could get lucky. Someone might remember seeing Segal and Perkins together. At least we'd know we're on the right track."

"I'm going to call my contact with the FBI in San Francisco today," Christopher added. "He might be able to get one of his guys in Seattle to do the legwork and save us the trip."

"Meanwhile, what can I do?" Kline asked.

"Not much to do now, Ben," Monk said. "Maybe just quietly keep an eye on Segal. We have to make sure he doesn't get spooked and disappear again. We appreciate that you've had your guys discreetly looking after Trent in the hospital. Keeping tabs on Segal has to be discreet as well."

"Yeah, I've got some good guys I'll put on Segal. They won't be spotted. He's opening a restaurant in Juneau. He flies down there every couple of weeks. Can't do much about that. But if he leaves town, we'll know about it. And if he tries to get at Marshall again, we can stop that."

"What about here in Anchorage, Ben?" Monk asked. "Anything out of the ordinary recently?"

Kline frowned.

"I hate this kind of thing," he said. "We don't want to say anything but we might have a serial killer on our hands. A maid in one of our rent-by-the-hour hotels found a body this morning. This is the third one. They show up about every six months."

"Doesn't sound good," Monk said.

"This one is strange, Robert," Kline said.

"Serial killers are all strange," Monk observed.

"Yeah, but this one is even stranger than usual. In most of these cases it's a man offing women in some kind of kinky sex thing. There might be a sex connection in this one, too, but the first two victims were men. The DNA indicates the killer is a woman but we can't be certain. Then the body found this morning was a woman. Tough to figure."

"You're right," Christopher said. "That doesn't fit a pattern."

"Don't breathe a word of this, Christopher," Kline urged. "The last thing I need is a city full of panic-stricken people."

Monk and Booth both pledged their discretion and rose to leave. Monk stopped at the door.

"I just had a thought," he said, turning back to the chief. "Maybe there is something you can do."

Segal walked the few blocks to the restaurant just before noon. He liked to be around when both the lunch and dinner crowds began arriving. Playing host was what he enjoyed. He had Jayne and other staff to handle everything else.

After half an hour greeting arriving guests, he walked the short distance to the stairs leading up to his office. He noticed again the young woman with black and red striped hair as he passed the kitchen.

She intrigued him. Never more so than today. She turned away from him at an angle. From the side, he saw something he'd not seen in her before. Feminine curves. It occurred to him that she dressed to downplay what he now saw was an attractive body. Curious, he thought. Perhaps she might be worth getting to know.

He found Jayne at her desk as usual but looking haggard. She was chain smoking, lighting one cigarette with another.

"Are you all right?" he asked, not out of concern for her but rather wanting to be assured that all was well with his business.

"Yeah, I'm all right. Just couldn't sleep last night."

He nodded though he wasn't sure she was being truthful. He thought he would have to keep an eye on her.

The young woman never looked directly at Segal but always watched him from beneath lowered lashes. She saw him hesitate as he walked by the kitchen. She felt his eyes roaming over her body. So far, she had successfully avoided attracting him. With sudden perspicacity, she thought maybe she should stop avoiding him.

Following the success of Operation Den of Snakes, the FBI Special Agent in Charge for the San Francisco area was called back to Washington, D.C., with a significant promotion. Joseph Brady, the agent who had actually led the FBI contingent assigned to Booth's task force, was also rewarded by being named the new SAiC.

Christopher got the answer to his second question when he asked the first.

"I'd like to help you, Christopher," Brady said, "but we're stretched about as thin as we can get."

"What's going on, Joseph?"

"Smuggling like we've never seen before," Brady answered. "We're drowning in pirated goods."

"CDs? Movies and music?"

"Some of that but streaming movies and apps to download music cheap have made that market hardly worth the risk," Brady said. "We're seeing fake everything else. Designer fashions. Designer jewelry. Shoes. Ladies accessories. Everything you can imagine. All fake. Our good citizens are happy paying a quarter of the price a legitimate merchant would charge for the real goods. If they fall apart a few months later, it's no big deal. There's plenty more of the fake stuff for sale cheap. The big stores are screaming at us to put a stop to it."

"Is it just in the Bay area?" Booth asked.

"It's all up and down the west coast," Brady's replied. "This stuff is showing up everywhere. We're not sure where it's coming in. It has to be by water. Air and ground traffic are both watched too closely. The coast from the Canadian border to Mexico is fairly congested. But there are some secluded coves. The Coast Guard is patrolling but they can't be everywhere. Meanwhile we're working on land to figure out who's behind it all."

"Sounds like you have your hands full."

"More than my hands can hold," Brady said. "I'd like to help you, Christopher, but all my guys are working long hours now. Seattle's the same."

"It's not a problem, Joseph," Booth assured the federal cop. "I was being lazy. Trying to save myself some shoe leather. I'll get it handled."

The mood was more somber when the group gathered for the cocktail hour on the deck. Darcey brought out two bottles of Napa Merlot. Darcey remained subdued after her conversation with Dr. Shannon. She had been so optimistic that she would find Trent moved out of ICU. The disappointment visibly affected her.

64

Robert discussed his plan for their next step. His idea didn't improve her mood.

"I guess I'll be going to Seattle," Christopher said. "My FBI buddy tells me they have their hands full. He can't spare anyone to do our legwork."

"What's tying them up?" Robert asked.

"Smuggling. Fake goods. Everything from fashions and accessories to electronics. Even pharmaceuticals. Viagra. Lipitor. Plavix."

"Fake blood thinners and cholesterol medicine?" Nancy said, acrimoniously. "That's cruel. There are a lot of people who'll buy cheap drugs because they can't afford the prices the big drug companies charge. And they won't know they're taking fake pills. I hope Joseph catches whoever's doing this and shoots them. Then treat them with their own fake drugs."

Robert started to say something but stopped himself. Something Nancy said triggered a thought but it was elusive. He stared out over Cook Inlet trying to capture it.

Same day. Dimension unknown.

Trent thought he was alive. He was still connected to machines so he must be alive.

Nothing more had changed as far as he could tell. He couldn't open his eyes. He couldn't speak. He could hear. He could sense the presence of others.

He knew Darcey had been here earlier. Someone was with her. Another woman. He didn't know who it could be. Betty perhaps? It would seem logical that her mother would be with her.

He hoped Kelli was well. He knew Darcey, Betty, and Ivy would see that she was. He thought he was the only one injured. But he had no way of knowing.

His head felt different. It felt like he was wearing a hat. Why would he wear a hat? Made no sense.

He was tired. No, not tired. He was drowsy. It was hard to stay awake.

Drugs. They must have given him drugs to make him sleep.

Why did they want him to sleep?

Dimension still unknown.

July 14th

Bastille Day in Anchorage promised to be the warmest day of the summer so far though the sky was gray. The bright blue of the past few days was blotted by clouds, none of which threatened the city with cooling rain.

The specialty hospital, which had been treating Trent Marshall, had erected a podium in the lobby, complete with microphone. Five of the reporters in the room had added their own microphones. Three cameras were set up and ready when APD Chief Ben Kline entered the room. He was accompanied by Dr. Natalie Shannon. Conversation in the room stopped.

"Good morning, ladies and gentlemen," Kline began. "Thank you for being here. This is not a happy occasion nor is mine a pleasant duty."

He paused before continuing.

"It's my sad duty to inform you that a well-known visitor to our state has been shot. Pulitzer Prize winning journalist Trent Marshall was shot by an assassin in Juneau six days ago. Despite the heroic efforts of Doctor Natalie Shannon and her associates here, Mr. Marshall has not regained consciousness. It is becoming apparent that the odds of his survival are not good. My office is supporting the Juneau Police Department as it investigates this case."

"Do you have any leads, Chief?" was the first question.

"I would classify them more as theories at this point," Kline said. "Whoever shot Mr. Marshall was very good at his job."

"A professional hit?"

"I would say so," Kline responded. "We are approaching the investigation with that assumption. As you might imagine, that means a far more extensive search for the shooter."

66

"Were there any other victims?" was the next question.

"Yes, one other man was killed," Kline said. "His name hasn't yet been released as we're having difficulty finding his next of kin. I can only tell you the second man was not a resident of Alaska either. Now that's all I have. If you have any questions regarding the injuries Mr. Marshall suffered, Dr. Shannon will address them."

Darcey had refused to watch Chief Kline's press conference. She knew it was coming. She knew what he would say. She wouldn't watch him. She wouldn't listen to him. Nancy brewed a pot of tea. They sat together in the sitting room. In silence.

Robert watched the live performance on the television in his bedroom. Kline played his part well. Robert didn't like hearing the chief's words either. But he listened. He watched.

In his condo on Second Avenue, Jim Segal's day was starting out well from his point of view. He poured himself a second cup of coffee, sipping it contentedly. He had switched his television on to the national news network he watched each morning. He was surprised when the local television station interrupted with live coverage of Chief Kline's press conference.

Finally, as they often say in a different context, he felt closure. Now he knew. Apparently, Marshall had not died immediately. He had been brought to Anchorage but the specialists in brain surgery available here appear unable to save him. It's clear they expect him to expire without regaining consciousness.

Events were moving in the right direction for him. It was shaping up to be a Bastille Day worth celebrating.

Segal was feeling quite pleased with himself. When he made the decision to get into what he liked to think of as the import business, he sought out a different way to bring goods into the country. It was Alaska's secluded coves and small bays that set him on the path now proving to be successful. Traditional smuggling methods were risky. Large vessels unloading at commercial docks required too much in the way of personnel and bribes.

Ironically it was the *Nanuq* that gave Segal the idea of using "chartered" luxury yachts. The Hannigans pioneered that business a few years ago and, by all appearances, were doing quite well. They had no competition.

Segal wasn't interested in competing with the Hannigans. They could have the luxury charter business. He saw a strategy for bringing fake goods into the country with far less risk than traditional methods. Any competition with the *Nanuq* was nothing more than illusory.

At 82 feet, Captain Place's Dancer was the smallest of the luxury yachts working for Segal. Place was grateful to Segal for gifting him the yacht after its previous owner was killed. Place had changed the name and the flag under which it sailed. When Segal contacted him and offered his proposition, the grateful seaman agreed to establish Dancer as the flagship of Segal's illicit fleet. It was also the fastest. The only one, in fact, that could outrun a cutter, most of which could reach a top speed of twenty-eight knots, or about thirty-two miles per hour.

In addition to Dancer, the small fleet included Integrity, Bounty, and Justice. Segal found all three vessels' names amusing.

Integrity was a 175-foot yacht with five guest cabins and a crew of eleven. It was the second fastest but still could only reach a top speed of fifteen knots, or a little over seventeen miles an hour.

The Bounty, at 137 feet was even slower. It, too, had five guest cabins but a smaller crew of seven.

The slowest of all was the one named Justice. He thought the name appropriate as it was owned by a woman who got it in a divorce settlement. Her ex-husband originally named it after her. After the divorce she changed the name. With five guest cabins, it required only a crew of six.

He was considering offering to buy the Justice himself. It was a beautiful, old-fashioned vessel built in 1927 with lots of wood and brass and glass. He hoped the Coast Guard never took it.

All four vessels had passed Coast Guard cutters several times. The Coast Guard saw pot-bellied middle-aged men with their half-naked, young wives or girlfriends having cocktails on the deck when the weather was good or sometimes trolling for salmon or jigging for halibut. The guests on the yachts always waved at the passing cutters.

The Coast Guardsmen smiled and waved back, unaware that hidden compartments below all the decks were filled with smuggled goods, or soon would be. They were also unaware that the "guests" were all on Segal's payroll. Their job was to play the role of people with sufficient wealth to charter their own private cruises through Alaska waters.

68

The Coast Guardsmen were also unaware that the crews, and some of the "guests," were armed with Colt AR-15s, the semiautomatic, civilian version of the M16. The AR-15 was a legal weapon in Alaska.

The rifles were for defense against some of their less than trustworthy suppliers. The skipper and crew of each vessel understood they were to avoid getting into a shooting match with a Coast Guard cutter. The yachts would be seriously outgunned. Segal's worst nightmare was the vision of tracer rounds from the heavy machine guns of the cutters arcing over the water to stitch holes at the waterline of one of the beautiful vessels in his service.

The crews and "guests" of all four boats were under orders to surrender if the Coast Guard demanded it. If they couldn't outrun the cutters, they certainly couldn't out fight them.

Captain Hannigan called while Robert was driving Christopher to the airport to catch the flight to Seattle that Darcey had booked for him. He was calling to see how Trent was doing. Robert told him about Chief Kline's press conference.

"I'm sorry to hear that," Hannigan said. "Trent is a decent man."

"Are you still in Juneau?" Robert asked.

"No, we're not far north of the San Juans. Have to get back to Seattle and pick up another group of passengers. Had to cancel one trip because the Juneau PD wouldn't let us leave. I can't afford to have that happen too often."

"Is your business that competitive?" Robert asked.

"It is now," was the reply. "It didn't used to be. We were the only luxury yacht booking cruises through Southeast Alaska until about a year ago. Now there are at least four others doing the same thing. But we're holding our own against them."

Once again the fleeting thought Robert had been trying to retrieve flitted through his mind and out again.

The man who delivered their grocery order every day had just arrived when Hackett wandered through the kitchen. Ivy was in charge of preparing the evening's dinner. She was going through the items as the man unpacked the box to be sure she had everything she needed. She was planning Atlantic croaker, a popular salt water fish that thrived in the waters off the Louisiana coast, in a caper sauce. Hackett hadn't eaten so well in years. He might never want to leave New Orleans.

As she supervised the unpacking, Ivy spoke to Betty.

"I was busy this morning when Darcey called. Did you talk to her? Any changes up there?"

"Only that their friends Captain Booth and Sergeant Patrick arrived from San Francisco," Betty replied. "They're both good cops. I feel better with them there to help Darcey and Robert."

Hackett was salivating as he imagined the spectacular meal to come. He listened to the conversation with only half an ear. The delivery man was paying more attention but likely out of concern for the size of his tip.

Robert mixed gin and tonics for the cocktail hour, appropriate for the warm weather the city had experienced again that day. Conversation was muted. For dinner, they did something hardly ever done in the Marshall-Anderson household. They ordered delivery. A box of barbeque from a local restaurant popular with locals and visitors alike.

The delivery driver would have been alarmed had he known that when he answered the door, Robert's small but deadly Glock was in his pocket where he could easily bring it into play. To the right of the door, Nancy lounged with her .357 magnum close at hand. To the left, Darcey's single shot .410 handgun was nearby. Caution was the motivator in the Marshall-Anderson household.

July 15th

Christopher Booth had landed in Seattle late in the afternoon the day before. He checked into a hotel near the waterfront before going out for a stroll around the neighborhood. His real purpose was to become familiar with the territory in the event he was forced to make a quick fight or flight decision. It was an experience every cop knew and and dreaded. It was a decision that had to be made in seconds. Or less.

He located the Caduceous, the waterfront bar in which Warren Perkins had been known to spend his evenings when his ship was in its home port. Satisfied he had learned enough about the surroundings, he returned to his hotel. He called Robert to report in before ordering a room service dinner. He watched a mystery movie on television and fell asleep with the television on.

He awoke early to a clear blue sky. A pretty weather girl dressed more for a first date than a morning news show was predicting that it would be in the mid seventies. A beautiful day in Seattle.

And a beautiful day on the waterfront when Booth walked the short distance from his hotel. He was dressed in faded jeans, pullover shirt and deck shoes. It was too warm for a jacket. Fortunately, his shirt was long and heavy enough to conceal the Glock on his hip.

He found a cheap restaurant across the street from the Caduceous. Like the dive bar itself, the restaurant was a hangout for seagoing men. He ordered biscuits and gravy with sausage and asked the waitress to keep the coffee coming.

Booth took his time over a leisurely breakfast. It wasn't that the food was good. It wasn't. He ate slowly so he could watch the people coming and going from the Caduceous, which apparently began serving its own version of liquid breakfast early.

Having extended breakfast as long as he could without attracting unwanted attention, he left a decent but not extravagant tip for the overworked waitress. He spent the next two hours walking around the waterfront.

He saw the *Nanuq*, which had arrived some time during the night, and spent a few minutes studying it. It was a beautiful vessel. Booth had difficulty envisioning Trent lying wounded on the deck. It was a picture he didn't want in his mind.

He returned to his hotel intending to visit the Caduceous in the evening. Until then it was time to stay out of sight.

As was his habit, Segal arrived at the restaurant just before noon. After greeting all the guests as they streamed in for lunch, he headed toward the stairs and his office on the floor above. This time when he passed the kitchen, he stopped.

The girl with the multi colored hair looked like a new person today. He was right. She had been purposely dressing to hide a very feminine, very desirable body. So much so that the first time he saw her he thought she was a boy. That mistake wouldn't be made today.

She was wearing makeup, which he had never seen her do before. She was still in jeans but they were form fitting, showing feminine curves, and a tight-fitting top, displaying more curves.

She looked directly at him for the first time, showing her large, brown eyes and a smile that could be interpreted as seductive. Segal didn't know what prompted the change but he was drawn to her. He was also relieved. Segal had few phobias but, like many men in middle age, he feared becoming unattractive to young women. While he had never been interested in marriage or even in a long-term relationship, he did enjoy his lifelong success at seducing any woman he chose.

He smiled back at her, then continued on toward his office. It wouldn't do to act too quickly. He enjoyed being in control of the occasional trysts in which he became involved. An immediate response would give her the mistaken idea that she would be in control of whatever relationship developed between them.

Jayne Colombo looked like herself again. Whatever had bothered her the day before now seemed under control. That pleased him. He needed her at peak performance. While he didn't want to send her out on a hit he did need her to handle other business matters.

One of her responsibilities was the transfer of funds to pay the suppliers of their fake products. Jayne had experience in finance and was better with computers than was he. At least she was sufficiently proficient to use the machine to move money around. Along with her other talents, it was one reason he had brought her to Alaska.

When he went into the "import" business, he set up a system as he had learned from watching the late Scott Douglas. Douglas handled transfers for Rossi's alliance until he realized that one of the members was funneling money to radical Islamic terrorists. He refused to make the transfer. Rossi foolishly ordered the kidnapping of Douglas' husband, Miles Diaz-Douglas, to pressure the financier into adhering to his obligation to follow orders. Even more foolishly Darcey Anderson was caught up in the kidnappers' net. It was that mistake that led finally to the complete destruction of all four gangs that made up the Rossi criminal coalition.

Robert mixed the cocktails this evening. Rum and coke. The trio remained subdued, still reacting to Chief Kline's press conference.

Leaving Robert alone on the deck with his second cocktail, Darcey and Nancy went to the kitchen. They decided to divert their attention with making excellent food. The kind of food that Trent loved.

This evening it would be tapas. A wonderful Spanish dish called gambas al ajillo. Shrimp with garlic. Large shrimp cooked quickly over moderately low heat in a pool of excellent olive oil with a large handful of garlic, a hot pepper, and other spices. Nancy sliced a long, thin loaf of crusty bread into rounds and toasted them while Darcey kept an eye on the shrimp.

There was more of a chill in the air this evening. Robert joined them in the dining room for dinner.

It was again late in New Orleans when his contact there called. Segal was pleased to know that the infiltration of Trent and Darcey's New Orleans home continued undiscovered. Speaking softly, he asked the contact about the general mood in the house. Did the occupants appear sad? Did they appear to be grieving?

The knot that was beginning to grow in his stomach felt larger when he heard the answer. All seemed to be well, the caller reported. As far as his contact could see, the inhabitants of the house were relaxed, even enjoying themselves.

Segal felt the fury raging within when he ended the call. What was going on? If Marshall was dead or at least not expected to live, why wasn't his family grieving? Would Darcey have not told her mother, at least, that Marshall would not survive? Perhaps she didn't want her daughter to be told until she was there. Kelli would want her mother when she was told her father was dead. But no, that couldn't be it. Someone was playing him for a fool.

It was a game that two could play. He stared out the window as one idea after another thumped through his mind like the Gregorian chants he endured in the Catholicism of his youth.

Booth waited until nine o'clock to enter the Caduceous. He wanted to allow time for the regulars to have a few drinks. They might talk more freely if their tongues were oiled.

He ordered vodka on the rocks from the woman tending bar. He would have preferred a martini but this wasn't the kind of place for that. The seamen who hung out at the Caduceous wouldn't trust anyone ordering a martini.

The bartender slapped the glass down in front of Booth, splashing some of the clear liquid onto the filthy bar, and walked off without bothering to wipe it up. It was going to be a long night.

He spent the next hour nursing the drink. In that time, he learned only that the bartender's name was Sharon. She didn't tell him. He heard one of the regulars call her Sharon. He learned that she didn't like anyone, especially Christopher, and that if he pressed her, she might be able to whip him. Booth was a big man. Sharon was bigger.

He tried to talk to her. He told her he was new in town. He said he had an old friend he was hoping to meet up with. Warren Perkins.

"Warren told me about this place," Booth lied. "He said if he was in port, he'd be here. Do you know him by any chance?"

"I don't ask people their names," was the burly bartender's only reply.

An old man two stools over at the bar showed Booth a toothless smile after the bartender walked away.

"Don't mind her," the old man said. "She don't like nobody."

"Yeah, that's what she said."

The old man looked down at his empty glass, then looked at Booth again hopefully. Booth got the hint.

"Can I buy you a drink?"

"Thanks," the old man said, happily accepting. He waved his empty glass at the unfriendly bartender as he moved over to occupy the stool next to Booth. Sharon shot an angry look at the old man but poured another shot of amber liquid into his empty glass. Booth held up his glass for a refill as well.

"I'm Chris," Booth said, holding his hand out to his new drinking buddy. The old man shook hands with fingers so fragile Booth was afraid he might break one or two.

"You can call me Disher," the old man said.

"OK, Disher."

"Are you a cop?" Disher asked.

"What? Why would you ask me that?" Booth scoffed.

"I don't know. You just look so healthy," Disher said, the thin skin of his face crinkling as he tried a nervous grin.

"That's what happens when you work the docks for a living. It's a healthy life."

Disher looked over at Sharon. The bartender was flashing a warning with her eyes. Disher looked down at the bar. When she went to the far end of the bar to pour another drink, he spoke softly without looking up.

"Finish your drink," he said. "Wait twenty minutes, then meet me outside. I might be able to help you."

Disher tossed back his drink, draining the glass. Sliding off the stool, he stood on shaky legs, steadying himself with one hand on the bar.

"I gotta be going, Chris," the old man said. "Sure nice to meet ya. Thanks for the drink."

"Anytime, Disher," Christopher said. "Maybe I'll see you here again."

"Yeah, maybe," Disher said as he shuffled out the door.

When Booth turned back, he was surprised to see the bartender slipping a semiautomatic from her back pack and stashing it under the bar. Another Glock. A little smaller than Booth's own.

Booth nursed his second drink for what he judged to be another twenty minutes. He drained the glass and slid off his own stool. He walked to the end of the bar to the filthy restroom. Inside he reached for the Glock on his hip to slide a cartridge into the chamber. With the safety on, he slid the weapon back into its holster, making sure to leave it loose in the event he needed it quickly.

"Guess I'll be going. Nice talking with you, Sharon," he said, with more than a little sarcasm, as he walked toward the door leading to the street.

"Yeah, I been havin' just a real good time," was the acid-toned reply.

Booth was glad to breathe in the cool, night air of the Pacific as he left the stink of the bar. Disher had something to tell him but was afraid to talk in front of Sharon.

The big cop wasn't sure where Disher was. He also wasn't sure he could trust the old man. He suspected Disher was looking to score a few bucks and could be helpful. But he had been a cop for a long time. He was cautious. The Glock on his hip was ready if it was needed.

Halfway down the block to his left he saw the shape of a man emerge from the shadows of an alley. A self-service laundry, closed, and a store selling marine supplies, also closed, stood between the Caduceous and the alley. Booth strolled leisurely in that direction.

Disher had stepped back into the shelter of the dark by the time Booth reached the alley. His bony hand reached out to grab Booth's sleeve and pull him deeper into the darkness.

"You want to know something about Warren Perkins?" Disher said, sounding considerably less drunk than he had appeared when he left the bar.

"Do you know him?"

"I know him. But a man has to eat, ya' know," Disher said.

Booth was expecting the request. He reached into his pocket and peeled two twenty-dollar bills from the roll he brought with him.

Disher looked a little disappointed but grabbed the bills quickly.

"I ain't seen Warren in a couple of weeks," Disher said. "He has a job as deck hand on one of the luxury yachts that charter out of here. But any night he's in port he'll be at the bar we just left."

Booth reached for his phone. His office had sent him a picture of Pietro Greco, aka Jim Segal, via text. The light from the phone was enough for Disher to see the picture clearly.

"Did you ever see him with this man?"

"I think I need to eat more than $40 worth," Disher countered.

Booth peeled off three more twenties but held on to them, waving them slightly in front of Disher. He returned the rest of his bankroll to his pocket.

"Yeah, I seen Warren with that guy. They were in the bar together maybe three or four times a few weeks before Warren's ship sailed."

Booth held the three bills out. Disher grabbed them.

"You got more of those twenties, don't ya?" he said.

"I got all you need, Disher."

"If you need any more information, I'll see what I can find out. I'll be in the bar every night," he said. He hobbled off down the street as fast as his old legs would carry him.

In Southeast Alaska, Captain Place was overseeing the transfer of cargo from a vessel registered in an Asian country. Crates of fake fashions, shoes, and handbags were stowed in the hidden compartments under Dancer's decks.

Cameron McGraw stood beside Place watching the activity. He had cruised south in the thirty-five foot Sea Ray Sundance that Segal kept berthed in Juneau. He did a little fishing along the way for show more than anything else. Fishing bored him but it was a necessary distraction.

When the transfer was complete, both larger vessels raised anchor and slowly left the small cove. McGraw pointed the bow of his smaller vessel toward the entrance to the cove and shoved the throttle forward. He quickly circled to the south of Prince of Wales Island until he was in range of the mobile towers in Ketchikan.

He made a quick call to Anchorage to report that the mission had been successfully carried out. Then he steered his boat into another small cove, dropped anchor, and, after positioning the fully loaded, cut down Remington 870 shotgun near his berth, went to bed.

Same Day. Dimension Unknown
Nothing had changed since the last time Trent became aware.

And everything had changed.

He was still unable to open his eyes or speak. He was aware. Only aware. But there was more. His damaged brain struggled to describe the sensation.

Swirling.

Whirling.

Spinning.

No, that wasn't it.

Close. Not quite it. But close.

He felt a presence in the room. He heard a familiar voice.

"Hey, partner."

"Joey?"

Trent was ten years old when he met Joey Costa. Trent and his mother had moved into a small house. Trent remembered thinking it felt like a huge mansion after the cramped little apartment they first lived in after Trent's father left.

The house was in a new neighborhood. It was summer. Trent would be going to a new school in the fall. He didn't have any friends in this part of town. The new house had a large yard. Trent played alone day after day. There were two boys near his age across the street. He waved to them but they ignored him.

One day Joey stopped his bicycle on the street by Trent's house.

"Hi, I'm Joey," he said.

Even then Joey was an outgoing young man, not given to the shyness, the victimology so prevalent among children his age. Trent and Joey were best friends since that day.

The first phase of their friendship lasted for three years. Joey's family moved to Alaska. The boys tried to stay in touch but the distance was too great. The short attention spans and insecurities and excitement of teenage years interfered. They lost touch.

When Trent's dad began taking him to Alaska for short visits, Trent and Joey reconnected. As adults they maintained their long distance relationship and visited when they could.

The friendship was again cut short when Joey died unexpectedly of a heart attack while skiing. It was the winter before Trent met Darcey. It added to the burden of guilt Trent already felt from the series of losses he had endured in recent years.

"Am I dead?" Trent asked.

"I don't know," Joey said. "It's hard to tell."

"But you died."

"Yes, I died," Joey said, with no trace of emotion.

"I saw my dad," Trent continued. "Dad was here. And now you. If I'm not dead, how can I see you and Dad?"

"I don't know," Joey said.

The two old friends were silent for long seconds. Trent broke the silence.

"I miss the fireworks."

Joey laughed.

As adults both had prospered. Joey was known in Anchorage for the spectacular, and highly illegal, fireworks display he hosted on New Year's Eve. Each year he spent several thousand dollars attaching the launchers to two sleds, which were linked together and dragged down from his house, which sat atop a steep hill, to the frozen lake below. At midnight, Trent and Joey would make their way through the snow to set off the first of the fireworks.

They stayed on the lake while Joey's guests watched from his house at the top of the hill. It was a spectacular show as one burst of color after another lit up the cold, clear sky over the lake.

"Hey, do you remember that time we were almost arrested?" Joey asked.

"Yeah, we looked up and saw two cops standing at the top of the hill looking down at us. You asked me what I thought we should do."

"And you said we should do nothing," Joey said. "I was sure the cops were going to come down and arrest us."

"Well, we were standing on a frozen lake with fireworks going off all over the place. We couldn't exactly plead innocent. But I knew they weren't going to arrest us."

"How could you be so sure?" Joey asked.

"Human nature, Joey," Trent said. "We hauled those heavy sleds down the hill but there was no way I was going to haul them back up. If the cops were going to arrest us, they had to take the evidence. That means they had to drag the sleds up the hill. I was pretty sure they wouldn't do that anymore than I would."

The two old friends had a laugh.

Then they were silent.

After a while, Joey began to fade away.

"Wait, Joey," Trent called out. "Don't go."

"It's not up to me, Trent."

"First Dad. Then you. I don't understand."

"I don't either. Not really. It isn't necessary to understand. Whatever it is will be ok. It'll be ok."

Joey faded away.

The swirling sensation returned.

Then it faded, too.

Dimension still unknown.

July 16th

Darcey sat on the couch in the large living room staring morosely into her coffee mug. She wasn't proud of herself. She was despicably failing to care for either her husband or her daughter.

Robert came out of the kitchen with his own mug. He stood for a moment, watching Darcey.

"It's not your fault, Darcey," he said softly. "You're doing what you need to do. What you have to do for now."

"I should be with my husband and my daughter.

Her response was in a monotone.

"I agree with that," Robert said, calmly. "But for now you can't be. It wouldn't be helpful to either of them. It will seem like forever but I promise it won't be long. What they need for now is for you to stay with our strategy. They need you to be strong. Trent and Kellie are both strong. So are you. It's who you are."

Darcey managed a small smile.

"Are you still with us?" Robert asked. He knew the answer. He wanted to hear her say it. He wanted her to hear herself saying it.

Darcey nodded.

"I'm still with you," she said, even managing a small smile.

Segal enjoyed his usual two cups of morning coffee and made two decisions. One decision per cup.

With the first cup, he decided it was necessary to flush Marshall's family out of their New Orleans fortress. He wanted them where he could get to them if he needed to use them for leverage.

Marshall wasn't his immediate concern. He was either dead or he wasn't. There were no other options. The bigger concern was the second part of the report he received the night before. His worst nightmare had come true. The Bay area cops Christopher Booth and Nancy Patrick had arrived in Anchorage. They could identify him as Pietro Greco.

What to do about them was far more troubling. It was one thing to kill Trent Marshall. He was a civilian. Booth and Patrick were cops. Killing cops wasn't smart.

There was also Darcey Anderson and Marshall's friend from Juneau. He might send Jayne to take one or both of them out. Or perhaps assign her to eliminate Booth? Let her be the cop killer?

There was danger in that if she turned on him to make a deal for herself. He didn't think she would do that. Murder wasn't a job for her. She needed to kill the way other people needed food or alcohol or tobacco or drugs. No, he didn't think she would turn. But it could happen. Should he risk it? The law said whoever hires a killer is a killer.

These were decisions for another day.

With the second cup, he decided that he would seduce that girl who worked in his kitchen. What was her name? Fiona. Yes, Fiona. Fiona Robinson.

But it wouldn't be smart to do it here. Juneau would be better. Maybe even on the boat. He would get her to go with him to Juneau by offering her a better job at JS Bistro Southeast. He felt himself becoming aroused at the thought.

He didn't feel he was facing any apocalyptic moment. There was no rush to implement either decision. He would give instructions to his New Orleans contact when he got the usual evening report. It would take a few days to put a plan in motion down there.

As to Fiona, no hurry there either. He was due to go back to Juneau in a few days. That would be the time.

Fiona's father always told her to pay close attention to the news. It was important, he said, to know what was going on in the world and how events would affect business.

Fiona had watched Chief Kline's press conference. Though he wouldn't know her, she knew who Trent Marshall was. She had seen Christopher

Booth and Nancy Patrick when they came to the restaurant. She knew who they were, too. She had no love for any of them. She might turn her attention to them some day. But for now, she was focused on Jim Segal. He was first.

She recalled that Segal was in Juneau on the day Marshall was shot. Could he have been the shooter? It would make sense if he was. Marshall could have caused him great misery had they run into each other.

There was a connection between Segal and Marshall from their time in San Francisco. It seemed illogical that there would be a third person in Southeast Alaska with a similar connection. Juneau was not a big town.

Her suspicion that Segal might have been the shooter was one reason she decided now was the time to let him seduce her. Or more appropriately, let him believe he was seducing her. She had her own plan for Jim Segal. She was ready to begin.

Robert dialed Captain Hannigan's number. He had captured the thought that eluded him the day before. Hannigan answered on the third ring though the connection was less than clear.

"Eric, when we talked last you mentioned that four other luxury yachts suddenly appeared in competition with you. It was like overnight, you said."

"Yes, they came out of nowhere," Hannigan said. "One day we were the only yacht in the market. The next day there were four others."

"Can you tell me their names?"

"Sure. Dancer, Integrity, Bounty, and Justice."

"Interesting names," Monk said. "Do you know who owns them?"

"They're all owned individually but as far as I can tell they work together. Maybe a single booking agent for all four or something like that."

"Are they also based out of Seattle?" Monk questioned.

"Out of this area," was the reply. "But I don't think they operate from the Seattle waterfront. I don't know for sure but I think they probably harbor somewhere in the San Juans near Seattle."

"Strange that there are four yachts doing business out of the Seattle area and you haven't seen them at the waterfront."

"Yeah, I've been puzzled by that," Hannigan said. "There's something else I think is funny. We advertise in several publications and various other media for customers. I've never seen an ad anywhere for the other four. It's like they come out of nowhere, find clients out of nowhere, and sail back into nowhere."

The conversation gave Monk more puzzle pieces. He didn't yet know how the pieces fit together. But a puzzle couldn't be solved until all the pieces were visible. They were starting to appear.

"So we have a definite ID of Segal meeting with Perkins in a Seattle bar," he said.

Nancy had put Christopher on speaker when he called in. He intended to report his findings but wanted to let Nancy know first that he missed her. Now Nancy, Robert, and Darcey were gathered at the dining table, hovering over the phone.

"How would he know that Trent and Darcey chartered the *Nanuq*?" Robert questioned.

"I've always had great respect for Greco's intelligence," Christopher replied. "He plays life like a chess game. Always thinking several moves ahead. He's smart enough to take good care of a few well-placed informants in the Bay area."

"Cops?" Robert asked.

"Maybe. Don't forget that one of our deputy chiefs was on the Rossi payroll and so was a detective in my own squad. There could be cops keeping him informed or others in key positions. Maybe at the docks. He's good at finding corruptible people. It didn't take him long to enlist Perkins."

"He came cheap," Monk said. "No doubt Segal always planned to get rid of him. When Perkins stepped out on deck that day in Auke Bay it was a bonus shot. "

"But Seattle? Why would he have people in Seattle?" Nancy asked. "Does he have business there?"

"He's in the restaurant business," Darcey said, thinking out loud. "Maybe he has suppliers in Seattle."

"I think there are several facts we should consider," Robert said. "First, Segal was in Juneau when Trent was shot. I saw him there that day."

"You think Segal is our shooter?" Christopher asked.

"Maybe," Robert said. "Segal is opening a second restaurant in Juneau, giving him a reason to be in Southeast often. He keeps a boat in Juneau.

When he's there, he and McGraw, his Southeast manager, take the boat out most weekends. If Segal isn't in town, McGraw sometimes goes out by himself. But my fisherman friends tell me they never come back with any fish."

"Maybe they're just not very good fishermen," Nancy offered.

"It's Southeast Alaska," Robert said. "The fish are so thick you can walk on them. In fact, I did step on some once when I was trying to cross a river. Anybody can have an off day, but no, if you consistently don't bring home fish you're not trying."

"Really?" Nancy asked. "You really stepped on fish?"

"This is Alaska. There are a lot of fish," Robert stated. "Hannigan told me that when he first put the *Nanuq* up for charter he had the market all to himself. Then almost overnight there were four similar vessels working Southeast Alaska."

Robert had their full attention.

"Earlier today Hannigan told me he hasn't been able to find out where the other four boats charter from. And he's never seen an ad for any of the four.

"Finally, Hannigan told me the day I met him that he got the idea for going into the charter business when he noticed all the secluded coves and small bays. Perfect for rich people who want to relax in privacy."

"Or crooks who want no one looking," Nancy interjected.

"And the FBI is seeing more counterfeit goods coming into the country than ever before. A lot of coincidences," Christopher said, drawing a look from Robert.

"Yeah," Darcey chimed in. "We know. There's no such thing as coincidence in crime, corruption, or politics."

"OK. Where do we go from here?" Christopher asked.

"I think you should stay in Seattle for a while longer, Christopher," Robert said. "See if you can find out anything about the four vessels Hannigan named for us. That guy you met in the bar. What was his name? Disher? Was that it? He might be helpful."

"Yeah, Disher. I'll see what else I can get out of him. He's in no shape to work the docks anymore. He needs cash and he sees most everything going on at the waterfront," Christopher said.

"I have a hunch about what Segal is up to," Robert continued. "I think I need to go down to Juneau and talk to the Coast Guard commander there."

"What about us?" Nancy asked. "What should Darcey and I do while you guys are gone?"

"Watch each other's backs," Robert said.

Segal had changed into his tux for the evening crowd. He loved the image of the successful restaurateur. He also liked the way he looked in a tux.

Glancing into the kitchen, he unequivocally knew Fiona thought so, too. She was wearing jeans again. They were skin tight and her top was revealing when she leaned forward, as she did now. His eyes were drawn to the soft, rolling hills and gentle valleys of her body.

Her eyes brushed across his when she looked up but she quickly lowered them under his dominant gaze. That pleased him. He would speak to her soon.

The luxury yacht Integrity was leaving a small dock in the San Juan Islands, its bow pointed north. Another group of "wealthy guests" were making an unavoidable show of having the time of their lives. After slowly cruising along the Canadian coast to reenter U.S. waters near Ketchikan, the guests would spend the next few days sunning themselves, weather permitting, and fishing for halibut and salmon.

The Integrity had a late night appointment for a rendezvous in yet another secluded cove on the 22nd to take on a cargo of sports shoes, sunglasses, and perfumes. All with designer names and logos. All counterfeit.

This was Segal's favorite kind of cargo. Small items. Light weight. Easily hidden in each vessel's secret compartments.

Robert opened a bottle of Mumm's Napa Brut Prestige, Trent's favorite wine. He sat on the deck with Darcey and Nancy, watching the light settle behind the Sleeping Lady.

Nancy and Christopher lived in an apartment in Richmond, the community just outside of San Francisco where Nancy had been on the police force until she quit to answer Darcey's call. Neither Nancy nor Christopher was talented in the kitchen. When they were home they often ordered pizza or picked up take out or dined on simple dishes. Scrambled eggs and ham sandwiches were big on their menu.

After serving as sous chef for both Trent and Darcey many times, this evening Nancy took charge of dinner for the first time. A ground turkey and rice casserole with sautéed onion, roasted red peppers, celery, mushrooms and fennel.

"I know casseroles aren't sexy," Nancy said, "but it's my first solo run. So be gentle."

"I think casseroles are great," Robert said. The truth was ground turkey, in Robert's opinion, was on a par with boneless, skinless, tasteless chicken breasts. He didn't consider either food fit for consumption. But he wanted to encourage Nancy's effort. "They provide multiple meals. I like that. Cook once. Eat three times."

"And they can serve as the basis for other creations when you gain confidence and get more creative," Darcey said.

"Well, tonight you guys are my guinea pigs. If you don't die of food poisoning, maybe I'll start cooking for Christopher."

In Seattle, Booth spent two hours with Disher at the Caduccean. The bartender wasn't pleased.

It was again late in Louisiana when Segal got the call from New Orleans. He explained what he wanted to happen. As he expected, he was told it would take a few days to set it up.

He was fine with that. He knew finding two expendable people was a delicate assignment. As things stood now, he could afford to be patient.

July 17th

Robert took a morning flight to Juneau. Living most of his life in Alaska, he had spent many hours in airplanes. He never told anyone he hated flying. He never let anyone know flying was one of the few things he feared.

Flying into Juneau was especially challenging. When the weather was good the flight pattern was over what was eerily called "the cut." It was a section of a knoll on which the trees were trimmed to create a clear approach to the airport. That alone was sufficient drama. But after crossing over the cut, the plane banked sharply to the right to line up with the runway. Robert hated to be seated on the starboard side. From there it appeared the wing tip would be dragged through the mud.

Taking off in good weather wasn't bad. But under certain weather conditions the airlines had been known to use an FAA approved procedure that Monk considered only slightly shy of insane.

The aircraft would take an immediate sharp left turn on takeoff, pointing its nose directly at the mountains. Within a few seconds, the pilot would make an equally sharp right turn, simultaneously cutting the engines. The long metal tube full of passengers would float silently as the airplane glided into position. It was only when he heard the engines come back to full throttle that Monk allowed himself to breathe.

He drove up to his house feeling as though he had once again cheated death thanks to a competent pilot. The mailbox was crammed full, mainly with junk. A few bills that had to be paid. No letters. No one wrote letters anymore. Not since the blessing and the curse of e-mail were foisted onto the world.

He tossed the bills on the desk in his small office and threw everything else into the trash. He hadn't bothered to bring a bag. He was going back to Anchorage soon and had done his own laundry there before leaving for Juneau. He had plenty of other clothing here.

He found the number for the Coast Guard commandant. Captain Jameson Van Patten had recently assumed command. Monk hadn't met Van Patten but he knew Master Chief Andy Mannix well. He had no problem making an appointment to meet with the new commandant at two o'clock.

In Anchorage, Nancy was doing her best to help Darcey stay positive. It wasn't easy. Darcey seemed always to be on the verge of tears.

When Darcey left to take Robert to the airport, Nancy had gone to her room to shower and get dressed for the day. She heard Darcey return. Then silence.

Coming out of her bedroom, she found Darcey sitting at the dining table. Staring at nothing.

She went into the kitchen, returning with two mugs of coffee. Placing one in front of Darcey, she sat down at the table with her own mug.

"It's not easy," she said, softly.

"You can't imagine what it feels like," Darcey said.

"I don't have to imagine. I know."

Darcey looked at her, surprised.

"Yeah, Christopher got himself shot a couple of years before we met you guys," Nancy said. "He took two rounds to the chest. He almost didn't make it. That was the worst time of my life. I could only sit beside his bed and watch him. Hoping he would keep breathing. Then one day he opened his eyes and smiled at me. I knew it was going to be all right. And that was the best day of my life."

"How did you do it?" Darcey asked. "Where did you find the strength to keep going?"

"I don't know. You just do. That's all," Nancy said. "Robert was right, you know. You're very strong. And Trent is as tough as they come. It's why the two of you were attracted to each other."

"Some days it seems overwhelming."

"Yeah, the load can get pretty heavy," Nancy agreed. "Christopher and I are both cops. We go to work every day not knowing if we'll ever see each other again."

"I don't know if I could do that."

"Are you kidding?" Nancy sounded incredulous. "Christopher and I deal with the threat every day because that's what we do for a living. You're married to Trent Marshall, who does it for fun. And you said yourself the other day that won't ever change."

That got a small laugh from Darcey.

"You're right about that," she said. "I'm married to an adrenaline junky."

"And you're as hooked as he is now," Nancy laughed. "You'd have a hard time living with anyone else."

Monk arrived at the federal building a few minutes early. He wanted to visit with Master Chief Mannix, who he hadn't seen in quite a while. They spent a few minutes talking fish. It was always the thing to talk about when two Southeast residents got together.

At promptly two o'clock the door to Captain Van Patten's office opened. The new commandant of Coast Guard Juneau stepped through the door, his hand outstretched.

"Colonel Monk, it's a pleasure to meet you," Van Patten said, as Robert rose and took the offered hand. "I've heard a lot about you since I have been in Juneau. You're something of a legend."

"The pleasure is mine, Captain," Robert said. "But don't believe everything you hear. And I haven't been called colonel in a long time. Robert will do."

"Robert it is then. And I'm Jameson."

Van Patten was about Monk's size but with more of a barrel chest and a booming voice. He ushered Monk into his office and closed the door, motioning Robert to a sitting area across the room from his large desk. They each took a wing back chair.

"I envy you your name, Robert," Van Patten said, with a sigh. "So simple. Robert Monk. Try going through life with a handle like Jameson Van Patten. When I was a boy, I thought my parents must have hated me. You wouldn't believe how many times I came home with skinned knuckles and a black eye or bloody lip after some school yard bully made fun of my name."

Van Patten's self-deprecating laughter rang through the room.

Monk's first impression of the captain was positive. He thought Van Patten was multifaceted, highly intelligent and capable. A good man to have on your side.

"But Chief Mannix tells me you're here on serious business, Robert. What can I do for you?" Van Patten asked.

"I think the question is 'What can we achieve by working together?'" Monk replied.

For the next hour, Monk briefed the Coast Guard captain on the shooting of Trent Marshall and all they had learned since that day.

"So you think there's a major smuggling operation taking advantage of the seclusion of Southeast Alaska." Van Patten summarized.

"Seems to make sense," Monk replied. "We know there's a former Mafia underboss now doing business under an assumed name in Anchorage. He's also opening a restaurant in Juneau, which gives him a reason to spend time in Southeast."

Van Patten nodded.

"We know since Eric Hannigan and his wife started their luxury yacht charter business, four similar vessels suddenly showed up to compete with them," Monk continued. "But they don't seem to be taking any business from the Hannigans. And we haven't been able to discover where their home port is or how they attract customers."

"It sounds suspicious," Van Patten agreed. "But we have to have more than suspicion."

Monk handed Van Patten a slip of paper with four names written on it.

"If you can look into these we might be able to get more than suspicion."

Van Patten read the words Monk had written. He nodded confidently.

"I can do that."

Segal sent for the young woman with the black and red striped hair. She entered his office dressed in the same form fitting jeans and low-cut top. She was trolling. No doubt about that. Segal thought the hook was baited for him. That pleased him. The question was, "Who would catch whom?" It was the type of game Segal enjoyed. A game he always won.

Jayne Colombo also knew Fiona was trolling for Segal. The older woman sat at her own desk across the room. Her eyes flashed angry fire at the younger woman's back. She was chain smoking again. Lighting one cigarette with another.

"I've been watching you, Fiona," Segal said. "You're a hard worker. You've done a good job for us here as a prep cook."

Fiona lowered her eyes submissively. Segal liked that.

"Thank you, Mr. Segal."

"As you know, I'm opening a second restaurant in Juneau," he continued. "How would like to be promoted to line cook at that restaurant? It would mean a raise in your pay, give you more experience, and let you see another part of Alaska. Does that sound interesting?"

"Yes, sir," she responded, careful to keep the tempo of her words at an even beat. "I would be very interested."

"Good. I'll tell you what. I have to fly down there in a few days. How about coming with me? You can look things over, meet the manager, and make a decision. I keep a boat down there so we might even do a little fishing."

Across the room Jayne Colombo fumed. Yeah, she thought, there'll be some fishing. But who was the fisherman and who was the catch?

"I'd like that, Mr. Segal," Fiona responded with some hesitation. "The only thing is…"

"Is there a problem, Fiona?" Segal asked.

"No, sir, except I really can't afford to lose any pay and if I'm not working here…."

Segal laughed.

"Don't worry about that, Fiona. You'll get full pay. After all, it's a business trip."

Jayne Colombo lit another cigarette from the butt of the one she had smoked down only halfway.

Darcey made her afternoon call to New Orleans before Kelli's bedtime. It was heartbreaking to be parted from her precious daughter for such a long time. She knew there would be more weeks of separation before the ordeal was over. There was nothing to be done but tough it out.

At the cocktail hour, Darcey opened a bottle of Prosecco. The Italian answer to Champagne was a favorite of their late afternoon ritual. She poured a flute for herself and for Nancy.

The two women touched flutes gently.

"Bon temps," Darcey said, repeating Trent's favorite toast. Good times.

Darcey felt guilty that she wasn't visiting her husband in the hospital. But Robert had strongly urged her to stay away as part of their strategy to confuse their enemy. She was thankful that Nancy was here to help her keep up appearances.

Christopher sat on a stool taking an occasional sip from the vodka sitting on the bar at the Caduceous. It was nine o'clock before Disher stumbled in. He sat on a stool beside Christopher. Sharon, the bartender, glared at them with her usual anger. It was a ritual of the past few days in which all three played their roles.

Christopher bought a drink for Disher. Over the next two hours, he bought the old seaman two more. The big cop continued nursing his first drink for another hour, then reordered for himself.

Draining the glass of his third drink, Disher said he had to go. Christopher took another twenty minutes to finish his drink before he wished Sharon a friendly good night.

She grunted and glared at him.

The old man told Booth he found out that the yachts were using a deserted island purchased decades earlier by a wealthy man who planned to build a resort. He built a dock and warehouse but died before any construction was begun on the resort. His heirs thought it not worth their time. They promptly forgot about it in their zeal to spend the money left to them. It wasn't much of a port but it was all Segal needed.

The old man knew one of the crew working the vessel Integrity. He had a dangerous background, including piracy. He was, Disher said, a dangerous man to be around. He also said the "wealthy guests" chartering the yachts often seemed to include some of the same people sailing on different boats. And, he said, it was doubtful that any of them were really wealthy.

Jayne returned to the restaurant an hour after it had closed. She had left the company's bank ledger and wanted to do some work on it before coming in the next morning.

She was surprised to see a strip of light under the door. Segal might be there, she thought. Then the door opened.

Segal wasn't there. Jayne stepped quietly back into the shadows. She watched as the girl Fiona came out of the office and eased her way down the stairs. Jayne let her pass, saying nothing as Fiona left the building.

Upstairs in the office, Jayne looked around. She could see nothing out of place. Except perhaps her own chair. It seemed pushed back. Out of place. Not where she had left it earlier in the evening.

Had the girl been sitting at her desk? Had she managed to access her computer? Should she speak to Segal about the incident? Or should she try to establish a relationship of her own with the girl?

Same day. Dimension unknown.

Trent still couldn't open his eyes. He couldn't speak.

He was sitting at a bar, a flute of Prosecco in front of him. How could he be here? How could he order? How could he drink?

He glanced at the woman sitting to his left. The mystery deepened.

It was his mother's aunt. The same aunt who had made him wealthy through her will.

She didn't speak.

She didn't have to speak.

He understood.

"You've come for me, haven't you?"

She smiled.

"I'm not ready. I still have things to do. I have to take care of Kelli and Darcey."

The aunt smiled.

And faded away.

Dimension still unknown.

July 18th

The night before Christopher had sent a text to Robert giving him the name of the island used by the four yachts working for Segal. He then fell asleep with the television on. It was a habit predating Nancy. As a single man he always slept with the television on. He still did when one of them was traveling.

The Seattle morning news brought him awake quickly.

"Authorities are attempting to learn the identity of the victim. We're told that he was an elderly man, probably a former dock worker. There was no identification on the body. He was found early this morning by longshoremen on their way to work. One of the men said he knew the victim casually. He said the victim went by the name of Disher. But he didn't know if that was a first or last name, or perhaps a nickname.

"While a final determination awaits the conclusion of the medical examiner, Captain Anthony Nettleton theorizes the victim was killed by three shots in the back, at least one of which pierced his heart. They believe the shooting occurred sometime around eleven o'clock last night."

Booth realized Disher was killed only minutes after he reported what he had learned about the luxury yachts. He thought it likely the bullets the coroner would dig out of the old man would be nine millimeters fired from a Glock 17. He knew where that Glock could be found. He didn't think the killer would toss it.

Booth didn't bother making coffee. There would plenty at the station house. He called the main number for the Seattle Police Department and asked for Captain Nettleton. Twenty minutes later he was in a taxi on his way to Nettleton's office.

In Southeast, Integrity was making its way slowly up the east coast of Prince of Wales Island. They had four days to kill until they were scheduled to anchor in a hidden cove on the coastline of Kosciuska Island. Once a prosperous community, the island had been largely deserted since an environmental lawsuit shut down the logging industry, which had been its mainstay. Now it was perfectly suited for Segal's type of industry.

Segal hadn't directed McGraw to participate in this transfer. He liked to have the man who, through force of old habit, he thought of as his underboss, drop in on the cargo transfers only occasionally. It was good to remind the yacht owners that they were his employees. It was also good that they never knew when or if McGraw, and his shotgun, would show up.

If McGraw didn't appear, the captain would call Segal, each using throwaway burner phones, to report when he was in position. When he verified that their supplier had arrived with counterfeit sport shoes, sunglasses, and perfume, he would have Jayne transfer the funds. The transfer of cargo would begin as soon as the supplier saw the funds show in his bank account. Banking was done through friendly banks on a twenty- four hour a day basis so the process would be quick.

The pampered guests aboard the yacht would spend the four days eating, drinking, fishing, and having a good time. They would be friendly to every other vessel they passed.

Captain Anthony Nettleton was a competent cop. The kind of cop Booth understood and respected. When he told Nettleton he hadn't taken time for coffee before contacting SPD, Booth was led to a battered old breakfront book shelf. The coffee pot sat in the center section that protruded out from the side sections. Both cops filled mugs with coffee and got down to business.

"I think I can give you the killer," Booth said, much to Nettleton's surprise. "At least, I'm pretty sure I can tell you where to find the gun the killer used. If I'm right and the slugs are nine millimeters, they came from a Glock 17."

"A Glock 17? Half the policemen in this country carry that weapon. You're not saying a cop did this, are you?"

"No way. I saw a Glock 17 at the bar where I met Disher. A place called the Caducean."

"The Caducean," Nettleton said with a grimace. "One of the worst dive bars in this city."

"The night bartender's name is Sharon," Booth said. "She's not the friendly sort. One night I saw her take a Glock from the backpack she carries and put it under the bar. It's a little smaller than my Glock 20 so I'm guessing it's a seventeen. She has been keeping a close eye on Disher and me. By the angry glares she directed at us she didn't like the old man talking to me. He was clearly scared of her."

"Sounds like she could be a suspect."

"She's no pro. If she did the job, my bet is she's not smart enough to toss the Glock. To her it's valuable property that she wouldn't want to get rid of."

"We'll find out," Nettleton said, reaching for the phone. "The DA will get us a warrant and we'll get on it. Her shift probably starts at six o'clock. We'll show up at eight. Want to go along for the ride?"

"Wouldn't miss it for the world," Booth said. "Disher liked his booze more than he should. But he wasn't hurting anyone. In fact, he was trying to help us catch some bad guys. And I have a special relationship with Sharon."

"I'll bet you have," Nettleton said.

Booth just laughed.

Jayne made it a point to linger in the kitchen when she got to the restaurant. She didn't like the attention Segal was paying to Fiona. She didn't like it that Segal planned to take the young woman to Juneau. Jayne knew what that meant.

She was already beginning to feel the depraved urges that controlled her. It had been only a few days since the last time. It was far too soon to leave another victim for the cops to find. But her growing resentment of Fiona added fuel to the fires that burned within her.

More importantly, she had to find out what the young woman was doing snooping around the office in the middle of the night. The other stuff was infuriating but personal. Sneaking into the office was business. That was unacceptable.

Fiona felt Jayne's eyes on her. She focused on her work. She didn't want to talk to Jayne. Fiona didn't have a good feeling about the older woman.

"You've made quite an impression on our boss," Jayne said, doing her best to sound friendly. "Congratulations on your new position."

Fiona smiled nervously.

"Thank you," she said.

"We should get to know each other," Jayne continued. "Maybe have dinner some evening. Or least cocktails."

"Sure, I'd enjoy that," Fiona lied.

Monk was at the federal building again by mid-afternoon. It hadn't taken Captain Van Patten long to get the information the old cop requested.

"All four vessels are registered in the Marshall Islands," the captain said, handing over a sheet of paper. "Here are the names of the owners. We have reciprocity with the Marshall Islands under SOLAS, the International Convention for Safety of Life at Sea. That means there are minimal inspection requirements for the yachts to operate in U.S. waters as long as they carry fewer than twelve passengers."

Monk passed along name of the deserted island in the San Juan chain that Segal was using as a base.

"There's an abandoned dock and warehouse there," Monk said. "No one lives on the island. Perfect for Segal's needs."

"I can have a cutter cruise by."

"If I can suggest, Jameson," Monk cautioned, "it might be smart to use a very light touch for now. Let's not do anything out of the ordinary until we're ready to scoop up the lot of them. If one of your cutters or aircraft goes by in the course of a normal patrol, no problem. Same goes up here, if you agree. If they pass one of the yachts, you might instruct your people to wave and smile. If they can get pictures of the people on board without being obvious, great. If not, they can note their observations to you but nothing more for now."

Van Patten agreed.

"Are these yachts required to get any sort of U.S. license to charter?"

"No. The reciprocity allows them to operate commercially in our waters for eighty-four days annually," was the answer.

"Eighty-four days," Monk mused. "Twelve weeks. Four yachts. Roughly four weeks per month. Each yacht can make one trip a month, more or less. Nice numbers."

"Yes," Van Patten agreed. "Rather coincidental."

Monk repeated his mantra.

"There's no such thing as coincidence in crime, corruption, or politics, Jameson."

"By the way, that guy you asked about, Marshall's friend who was on deck with him that day, is Robert Monk," Cameron McGraw said. "He's a retired cop. He was a colonel in command of the State Troopers and later Commissioner of Public Safety. And he's back in Juneau."

Segal had called McGraw to tell him he was bringing Fiona with him the next time he flew to Southeast and he would be taking her out on the boat alone. He had asked McGraw to find out what he could about the man. What he was hearing now chased the leer from his voice.

"How do you know he's there? Have you seen him?"

"Yeah," McGraw replied. "Saw him yesterday when I was in the federal building. Looked like he was going into the Coast Guard commander's office."

Segal could feel himself going pale. Monk was a former cop. Not only a former cop but a very important former cop. Why was he talking to the Coast Guard?

The only possible answer to that question drew Segal to another decision. His plan to flush Marshall's family in New Orleans out of their fortress had to happen now. He needed them to be where he could get to them.

He would also have to talk to McGraw. Why hadn't the man reported this news to him the day before? Segal wouldn't abide that kind of incompetence.

In the penthouse overlooking Cook Inlet, Darcey was still having difficulty functioning normally. There was nothing normal about her life. Nancy was quick to point out that the current situation was only temporary.

The former detective sergeant also did everything she could to make her friend stay busy. Darcey was doing her best to follow Robert's advice that she stay away from the hospital for the time being. It wasn't easy. Nancy knew exactly the pain her friend was feeling. She tried to distract Darcey using every bit of chicanery she could think of.

The obvious distraction, and the easiest, was urging Darcey to continue Nancy's culinary education. Today they made chicken gumbo. Darcey had taught Nancy how to make a roux, the most critical part of gumbo. This was the first time she was going to try it solo.

As Darcey watched, Nancy stirred the flour and peanut oil to make a roux. She stirred. She stirred more. And she stirred still more. Finally the roux reached the desired deep mahogany color.

Darcey had taught her the spices to stir into the roux, letting them settle into the base before adding the other elements. Next came the Trinity, as it is called in Louisiana. Onion, green pepper, and celery. As the vegetables began to soften, Nancy added chucks of andouille sausage to let it brown. Then green onions and garlic.

They were using leftovers from a roast chicken Darcey had made earlier in the week. Adding that to the pot, along with some okra, and pouring in the stock they had made with the bird's carcass completed the active part. Now it was up to the gumbo to simmer for about two hours.

As they had worked right up to the cocktail hour, Darcey made peach martinis to celebrate her friend's accomplishment. Trent, Darcey told her friend, would be proud of her. He would have made peach martinis for them.

They sat on the deck on the west side of the building as had become customary. They were both still fascinated with the magnificent view of the Sleeping Lady. They couldn't see Denali today as it was far too cloudy. But this side of the building, as Robert had said, offered safety as well as view.

In Seattle, Captain Nettleton entered the Caducean, accompanied by six uniformed police officers and Booth. The plain clothes officer he sent in earlier had confirmed that Sharon was behind the bar. He remained near the bar to keep an eye on her. She was surprised to see the police. When a suspect is surprised, there is no way to know how they might act. She might do something foolish. She did nothing at first.

"Everyone stay where you are. We are only interested in one person here," Nettleton announced, as he walked to the bar. Sharon reached for something under the bar, causing Nettleton to draw the Korth PRS from its holster on his hip. "Don't reach for it, Sharon. Your Glock might have more cartridges in the magazine but I assure you I need only one."

Sharon proved she wasn't completely stupid by withdrawing her hand.

"Good decision," Nettleton said, keeping the Korth trained on the bartender as he spoke to the uniformed officer at the open end of the bar. "Officer, please use your cuffs. I'm sure Sharon knows how they work."

The bartender glared him as she put her hands behind her back.

The captain walked behind the bar and pulled the bartender's backpack from beneath the bar. Looking inside, he found a wallet containing her driver's license, reading her full name.

"We could have done this much easier, Sharon Bean, had you not tried to go for this," Nettleton continued as he reached into the bag again. Using a handkerchief, he withdrew the Glock 17, and dropped it into an evidence bag.

"You're under arrest, Sharon Beal," Nettleton said. "The charge is suspicion of murder. Officer, be so kind as to advise Ms. Bean of her rights."

As the officer went through the standard recitation of the Miranda statement of rights, the captain turned to address the handful of customers.

"Now I'm afraid I have to ask you all to leave," he said, "since we're taking the only employee with us, we'll have to lock the building to protect the property. And then, too, there is this," he said, waving the search warrant. "Please give your names to the officers who will be at the door, and I also must insist that you show them some identification. I apologize for interrupting your evening."

In the car on the way back to Nettleton's office, Booth congratulated him on how easily he handled what could have been a nasty situation.

"I also think Seattle must pay its cops a lot more than San Francisco," Booth said. "That's a Korth PRS you carry, isn't it? One of the world's finest, and most expensive, weapons."

"Yes, it is a fine weapon. As to its cost, it was a gift from my father when I was promoted to captain. He's already made his money."

Nettleton and Booth left the bartender to be booked and the Gunshot Residue test done on her hands and clothing, while the ballistics experts tried to get enough bullet fragments from the victim's body to link them to her gun. The two cops walked three blocks from the precinct office to a diner. They both ordered fried eggs over hash.

"No point in us going hungry," Nettleton said. "We're not going to get anything tonight anyway. The residue test isn't reliable, not even the newer Scanning Electron Microscopy. Any half way decent defense lawyer will get whatever we find thrown out as evidence. Chances are slim that ballistics will get enough of a bullet to be conclusive either."

"Maybe she'll do something stupid. Most non pros do. We probably couldn't solve near as many cases if they were all smart," Booth said.

"We'll try to bluff her and hope she watches a lot of cop shows on TV," Nettleton said. "But the state's moratorium on carrying out the death penalty makes that harder. She knows at worst she'll have to sit in a prison cell for a few years."

"So we'll hope for stupid," Booth said.

They were lucky. The bartender gave them stupid.

When they returned to Nettleton's office, a uniformed officer handed the captain an evidence bag. It contained three expended cartridge casings.

"Where did you find these?" Nettleton asked the officer.

"In her coat pocket, Captain," was the answer.

Nettleton looked at Booth. He could only shake his head.

"And Captain, her fingerprints are on all three. There's no doubt she loaded them into the magazine of her Glock, which is three rounds light."

"Anything else in the backpack?"

"Just this, Sir," the officer handed over another evidence bag, this one full of money. "$5,000."

"If only the crooks were smart…" Nettleton paraphrased Booth's earlier observation.

Nettleton motioned for Booth to follow him into the interrogation room in which Sharon Bean waited. He had ascertained that the bartender had been read her rights. She had not requested an attorney.

The Seattle cop opened the door and, for moment, he stared at the bartender. He tossed the evidence bag containing the three cartridge casings onto the table in front of her.

"Sharon, Sharon, Sharon," Nettleton said. "What were you thinking? You were smart enough to pick these up after you killed Disher and then you put them in your pocket? It didn't occur to you that you might be a suspect and we might search you?"

Sharon looked ill. Booth thought she might throw up. Then she made her situation worse.

"I meant to toss'em when I got off last night but I was tired. Guess I just forgot."

"That's a mistake that is going to cost you your life, Sharon," Nettleton warned. "Your fingerprints are all over them."

"It's just three casings. Just because I picked'em up doesn't mean I killed that old man. Anybody could have left them in the alley. Maybe I found'em and was trying to be a good citizen."

"Sharon, I have three expended cartridge casings with your fingerprints on them. The magazine of your Glock is light three cartridges. When we get the results of all the tests back we're going to find gunshot residue from your hands and clothes. We're going find the bullets that killed Disher came from your gun," Nettleton bluffed. "And Disher was scared of you. He just as much as said so to Captain Booth here."

"I knew you were a cop!" the bartender exploded at Booth. "I warned Disher to stay away from you."

"You need to understand, Sharon, that I have enough on you to convict you of murder," Nettleton said, drawing her attention back to him. "That's still a death sentence in this state."

"They ain't executing people in Washington," she said, morosely.

"There's a moratorium on carrying out executions, Sharon," Nettleton explained patiently as though speaking to a child. "The law is still on the books and losers are still being sentenced to death for murder. Especially if it's a murder for hire situation, which I somehow suspect this one is."

He tossed the evidence bag containing the money on the table.

"Any reason you thought it smart to carry this around with you?"

"I couldn't leave it at home. I got two roommates. They woulda stole it. And I ain't got no bank account."

"Well, you have yourself quite a massif to climb, Sharon."

She looked puzzled.

"What's a massif?" she asked.

"It's a mountain range," Nettleton responded. "And the one you have to climb is about as big as the Cascades."

"You stop using those big words. You're confusing me. That ain't fair."

"I'll tell you what else isn't fair, Sharon," Nettleton said, leaning dramatically forward. "It's not fair to sneak up on an old man and shoot him three times in the back. You're going to spend the rest of your life sitting on death row praying the moratorium is never lifted. That's not the way I'd like to spend my life."

The bartender didn't seem quite as tough as she had earlier. She seemed deflated. Defeated. She sat silently staring at the table. Nettleton let her stare.

Finally she spoke without looking up.

"What do you want to know?"

"Who paid you to kill Disher? And why did they want him dead?"

"A guy I know came to the bar. Gave me the money and said his boss didn't want Disher talking to this cop anymore. He wanted Disher out of the way."

"How did he know Disher was talking to Captain Booth?"

Sharon's answer was inaudible.

"Speak up, Sharon," Nettleton said. "I can't hear you."

"I called the guy. Told him I thought Disher was talking to a cop."

"What's his name, Sharon? Where can I find him?"

"His name is Kevin Donovan. He works on a boat somewhere around here. I don't know anything more about him."

"That's good, Sharon," Nettleton said. "That's very helpful."

"I had to do it," the woman whined. "If I didn't do what Kevin told me, he would have killed me. I figured I didn't have a choice so I might as well get some money out of it."

"I hope it was worth it for you, Sharon."

"So what are you gonna do for me?" she asked.

"I don't know if anyone can help you, Sharon," Nettleton said.

"But I helped you, didn't I?" she pleaded. "You just said so. Ain't that worth something?"

"We'll see. It might get you sentenced to life without parole instead of death. I'll see what I can do."

July 19th

"It's time for a summit meeting," Monk said.

Booth had called Monk from Captain Nettleton's office, reaching him at his Juneau home. The retired Alaska cop made his pronouncement after the three exchanged reports on Disher's murder, the bartender's arrest, and information gathered in both Seattle and Juneau.

"We're not simply trying to solve a single vicious act and bring one person to justice. The criminal activity that led to the shooting of Trent Marshall is systemic. It affects not only Alaska but Seattle, San Francisco, and perhaps the entire west coast."

The two younger cops listened as Monk outlined what he had in mind for his summit meeting and who should be involved. They would work together to organize the meeting. Each of the three was assigned names to contact based on their individual relationships. Monk would ask Van Patten to talk to his counterpart in Seattle. They hoped to determine a date and time for the meeting, which would be conducted mainly via telephone, as soon as possible.

Darcey's morning call to Kelli was especially unnerving.

"Mommy, when are you and Daddy coming to pick me up?" the child had asked.

Darcey's heart was breaking as she tried to answer the unanswerable question.

She felt helpless. She stared out the window and watched the drizzling rain fall.

It was midnight in New Orleans. James Hackett stood in the shadows behind the brick wall protecting the Marshall-Anderson house in the Vieux

Carre'. He wasn't surprised when he saw the smaller of the two faded green doors in the wall open. Nor was he surprised when the alarm failed to sound. It was the attack he expected, carried out in the manner expected.

He let the black-clad intruders reach the fountain in the center of the courtyard before he stepped out of the shadows.

"That's far enough," he said. His Korth Sky Marshal was trained steadily on the pair. The small nine millimeter revolver with its stunted barrel was not completely visible to Hackett's opponents. That was not his concern.

The pair turned toward him.

"Uh…We was told there wouldn't be no guard," one of them said, nervously.

"Looks like you were told wrong."

"Let's get out of here," the second man said.

"We got a job to do. There's only one of him. There's two of us," the first man said, raising the semiautomatic in his hand.

The second man followed his partner's lead. Both were unsure. Hesitant. That was a mistake.

Hackett fired four times. Each of the would-be assassins was hit twice. One in the chest; one a killing shot to the head.

Hackett walked over to the two bodies now lying crumpled on the bricks. He kicked a weapon away from each of two lifeless hands. Berettas. The latest version of the M9, he thought. A highly reliable weapon favored by the U.S. military. If he was correct, each magazine held seventeen nine millimeter rounds. Thirty-four rounds between them. Hackett had six. He didn't need all of them.

From the gallery he heard Betty call out.

"James? Are you all right? What's going on?" she called.

"It's ok, Betty. Keep Kelli inside. We had visitors but the trouble is over. I'm calling Jordan now."

In the courtyard, New Orleans police forensics experts were combing the courtyard. The medical examiner had taken the bodies away.

In the house, Jordan Baron sat in the kitchen with Betty and James. He was sound asleep when the call woke him but he came immediately awake when he heard Hackett's report. He was at the house on Governor Nicholls Street in less than half an hour.

"The alarm didn't sound when they opened the door?"

"Not a peep," Hackett said.

"Then they either had the code or they bypassed the system."

"It's not that hard to bypass a security system," Hackett pointed out.

"They also picked a time when the plain clothes officers I assigned to patrol the house would be away," Jordan added.

"Which they could figure out just by watching," Hackett said. "It's easy to fall into a routine with that kind of patrol duty. And routines are easily spotted."

Ivy was upstairs with Kelli. The child had hardly noticed anything going on. She was a sound sleeper. Ivy was sitting with her so she wouldn't be alone if she woke up.

Betty was showing the toughness of the Belmonts, her northwest Louisiana pioneer ancestors. She had also become accustomed to the action that surrounded her daughter's husband, and anyone around him.

"We all thought this would be the safest place for us," Betty said. "Now I'm wondering if anyplace is safe."

"We were trying to be low key," Jordan said. "That's why I didn't assign an entire squad to stand guard here. We thought a discreet patrol plus James would be enough. And I guess we were right since James handled the situation. How was it you were in the courtyard when they came in, James? Have you been standing guard every night?"

"Not exactly," James said, a little embarrassed. "At my age, Jordan, you don't sleep so well. I wake up in the middle of the night and can't get back to sleep. Since I've been here I've used those times to walk around the house and courtyard just to be sure all is well. That doesn't qualify me as a dotard though."

Jordan smiled at Hackett's refusal to be labeled senile.

"I'd say you're about as far from dotard status as anyone could be. It's too bad we didn't get one of them alive though. We might have found out who was behind this attack."

"I was outgunned, Jordan," Hackett defended his action. "I responded the only way I know how. Shoot to kill and worry about the consequences later."

"Can't argue with that," Jordan said.

"Any idea who they were?" Hackett asked.

"No IDs on them but we've seen these two before. They're a couple of small time wannabes. A job like this one was way out of their league."

"Someone armed them well," Hackett said. "The Berettas they carried are very good weapons. Not the kind of handguns you'd expect to find on the likes of them."

"Whoever sent these men has to be the same guy responsible for the attack on Trent," Jordan said. "I'm wondering how he tracked y'all here."

"Yeah, good question," Hackett agreed.

"And I'm wondering what we do now," Betty added.

"Trent would tell us we can't let the enemy be in control," Jordan mused. "They found y'all here and figured out how to get to you. I think we move. Give them something new they have to evaluate."

"Move to where?"

"How about to the Pines?" Jordan said.

"My farm? Do you think that's a good idea? It doesn't have a wall around it like this house."

"No, it doesn't, and two bad guys were able to walk right through the wall tonight," Jordan pointed out. "But your house sits on high ground and is defensible. Anyone attempting to attack the Pines has to either come up the easily blocked drive or cross open ground. We've got James, and Jack Blake will make available all the resources of the sheriff's department. And if that's not enough, I'm going along for extra coverage."

"Well, if you think so, Jordan," Betty complied.

"It'll be dawn soon," Jordan said. "I suggest we try to get some sleep. I'll leave a couple of men on duty in the courtyard. No point in trying to be discreet now. Let's use tomorrow to rest and get packed up. We'll leave on Friday."

Same Day. Dimension Unknown.

Trent Marshall felt the presence.

Not a warm presence as had been the others.

A dark presence.

A threatening presence.

"So you finally got it. Someone finally gave you what you deserve. I just wish it could have been me."

Trent knew that voice. He hadn't heard it in more than a decade.

Josh Blair!

When Trent's mother passed away, the boy went to live with his father in Baton Rouge. It was there that he met Josh. With Joey gone,

Josh became Trent's best friend. They were inseparable through high school and beyond.

The Blair family was among the richest in Louisiana. Their power was immense. Josh learned at an early age that he could do as he pleased. His family's money and influence would protect him. He marched through life like a feudal lord.

Trent knew Josh wasn't normal. He saw the way his friend mistreated, even humiliated, others just because he could. He tolerated Josh's behavior in silence, believing he had to be loyal.

Then came the day when he could no longer protect Josh. The day he discovered Josh was heavily involved in a corruption scheme Trent had uncovered. With great sadness, he watched as Sheriff Jack Blake arrested Josh at his lake house in Sabine Parish.

It was the story for which Trent won a Pulitzer Prize. It was the story that destroyed Josh and, eventually, his son. It almost destroyed Trent.

Trent still couldn't open his eyes. Couldn't talk. Yet he heard himself answering his friend.

"You're probably right, Josh," he heard himself say.

"My good friend," Blair sputtered, spittle flying from his lips. "You got me sent to prison. You knew I wouldn't survive."

"I would have prevented it if I could, Josh."

"Liar!" Blair shouted. "My blood on your hands wasn't enough to satisfy your lust. You had to kill my son! You killed Johnny!"

"Johnny was as deranged as you are," Trent replied. "He killed your wife, his own mother, Josh."

"Yes, with a knife," Blair raged. "A razor sharp blade to draw across her throat and yours as the prison thug sliced through mine!"

"When I shot him he was preparing to kill Darcey before he killed me. There was no way I would allow him to do that. I might have harmed you but Darcey never did anything to you," Trent said. "Johnny was no longer the little boy who called me Uncle Trent. He was a mad man."

"You made him that way!" Blair tried to shout again. But his voice was fading. He was fading

Trent was wiped out. So tired.

He was unaware of the degeneration of consciousness into darkness. Dimension still unknown.

July 20th

Darcey was shaken. Her morning call to New Orleans brought far more than heartbreak. It brought fear. Fear to the brink of panic.

The need to move strategically in a different direction was axiomatic. She was as surprised as anyone that her family had been found in the house on Governor Nicholls Street. She was even more surprised that the two striving assassins so easily penetrated their defenses.

"I'm going to Louisiana," she announced to Nancy.

"Do you really think that's a good idea?"

"What else can I do? My daughter is in danger," Darcey said. "She needs her mother and I'm three thousand miles away."

"Kelli has Betty and Ivy," Nancy pointed out. "And she has Robert's friend, Hackett, and Jordan Baron. When they get to Sabine Parish, she'll have Jack Blake and his army of deputies. I can understand how you feel, Darcey, but Trent needs you here."

"You can't ask me to choose between my husband and my daughter. I can't do that. It's not fair."

"No, it's not," Nancy replied, speaking as gently as she could. "But nobody ever promised fair."

Darcey's shoulders sagged in a gesture of defeat.

"I suppose you're right," she said finally. "But if Trent needs me, why am I sitting here? I'm going to the hospital."

"But Robert said…"

"I don't care what Robert said," Darcey interrupted. "I'm going to the hospital."

Dr. Shannon looked up as Darcey entered the room into which Trent had been moved.

110

"I thought you were going to stay away?" she said. "Didn't Colonel Monk say it was dangerous for you to be seen coming and going?"

"Yes, but I could only stay away for so long."

Dr. Shannon sighed. She was not pleased.

"I suppose I can understand that," she said. "But we also have to be concerned for the safety of our other patients."

"We'll be cautious, but I stayed away for as long as I could. Chief Kline has undercover men here standing guard. And I travel with my own armed escort," she smiled wanly as she tilted her head toward Nancy standing near the entrance into the room.

"Well, this is a good day for you to be here," Dr. Shannon said. "There's something going on in Trent's healing brain. I've just been going over the overnight monitoring reports. He had a period of several minutes last night when he seems to have been quite agitated."

"Oh, what does that mean? Is that bad?"

"We really have no way to know what it means. We monitor his brain functions constantly. So far his brain has continued in control of the important things, though he probably isn't aware of it," Dr. Shannon explained.

"What important things?"

"Bodily functions that we take for granted. Regulation of body temperature, blood pressure, respiration, heart rate, kidney functions, and production of hormones needed to make all those things work. Also all the senses," the doctor continued.

"The senses? Do you mean Trent might know if I'm here, might hear what I'm saying, even though he's unconscious?"

"That's an area of some uncertainty, but yes, it's possible," was the answer.

"Then like it or not, Doctor, you can expect to see me here every day," Darcey declared.

Segal was feeling good. The rain had stopped. The sun was shining. It promised to be another warm day. Warm by Alaska standards.

The report from New Orleans the night before was good. It was unfortunate that the two men sent to invade the compound on Governor Nicholls Street were killed. Unfortunate but not unexpected. The assault was not intended to succeed. The goal was to drive Marshall's family from behind their brick wall to a less secure location. That goal was achieved. The two assassins were not only incompetent, they were superfluous. There were many more like them.

He was looking forward to going to the restaurant today. He was enjoying the attention Fiona was giving him. The expectancy of taking the young woman to Juneau brought pleasure to his day. Even more so the thought of getting her alone on his boat, far from prying eyes and ears. He could almost feel the predictable euphoria in his imagination.

At JS Bistro on Fifth Avenue, two others were thinking of Fiona's coming trip to Juneau.

In the Kitchen, Fiona was imagining what it would be like to be on the boat alone with Segal. It was a moment she had anticipated for a long time. She was in no hurry for the point in time to arrive. She wanted to savor each minute leading up to it.

In the upstairs office, Jayne Colombo's eyes blazed when she thought of Segal and Fiona alone on his boat. He had never invited her to accompany him to Juneau, much less onto the boat. She would make him pay for the slight.

Christopher Booth landed in Anchorage in the late afternoon. Nancy had worked hard on a meat sauce for spaghetti. She used ground beef, mushrooms, and lots of spices.

Christopher mixed the martinis when the cocktail hour arrived. He spent some time telling them about his adventures in Seattle.

Darcey was feeling much better after seeing Trent. She would see him again the next day.

And the next.

And every day thereafter.

July 21st

It was hot when they left New Orleans.

It stayed hot as they drove north and west on I-10, then north again on I-49.

It was hot when they turned off the interstate at Lecompte for lunch at Lea's, famous for its ham sandwiches and pies. Kelli clapped her little hands when Betty and Ivy bought four pies, two chocolate and two pecan.

It was still hot when they arrived at the Pines in late afternoon. Jack Blake was waiting for them. Two of his marked cars, each with two deputies, waited with him. One blocked the entry into the long, winding drive up to the old house. The other was hidden from sight in the barn, the deputies assigned to watch the pasture on one side of the large building and the woods on the other. He had also stationed a car with two deputies at the old warehouse on the far side of the thick stand of trees bordering the rear of the large house. There had been mischief launched against the family from that warehouse in previous escapades.

"Welcome to the real Louisiana," Blake said, with a wide grin as New Orleans native Baron introduced him to James Hackett.

Baron laughed.

"That only means they don't allow go cups here, James," he said.

Hackett appreciated the friendly nature of the relationship between the country sheriff and urban policeman. He wasn't fooled by their light-hearted nature. They were fighting men. He had no doubt they would be formidable allies. Or enemies.

"Thanks, Sheriff, glad to be here."

A giggling Kelli ran past them holding a handful of carrots. She had insisted on stopping at a small town grocery store so she could

113

give the treats to Prince George and Mac, her mommy and daddy's horses, respectively.

"Hi, Sheriff Jack," she said as she ran by. "My daddy said I can have my own horse when I'm five."

"Hey there, Kelli," Blake called after her. "How old are you now?"

Grace held up three fingers without slowing.

"C'mon, Mamaw Betty," the little girl urged. "C'mon Mamaw Ivy. Prince George and Mac want their carrots."

The older women followed the child as fast as they could. A brown and white horse with the telling white legs of a tobiano paint and a bay trotted up to the fence enclosing the pasture to see what all the fuss was about. Prince George, the paint, and Mac, the bay, both nickered audibly as they recognized the small blonde head bobbing toward them.

The three men unloaded the Jeep while the women were saying hello to Prince George and Mac.

"You still favor that Herstal shotgun, Jordan?" Blake asked.

"Got it right here in this case," Jordan replied, as he lifted a long but otherwise inconspicuous duffel bag from where he had stowed it under the dashboard in the front seat. They wanted to keep the guns out of Kelli's sight but handy. Since Jordan was driving, Hackett made the trip with the bag beneath his legs.

"And I take it you're armed, James?" Blake asked.

Hackett was wearing a pullover, short sleeved shirt with the tail not tucked in. He lifted it to show the small but deadly Korth Sky Marshal holstered on his belt.

"How about you, Jack?" Jordan asked. "You still hauling that monster machine gun Homeland Security bought for you?"

"It's not a machine gun. It's a rifle with options," Blake corrected. "But yep. Got my M4 right there in the front seat."

"Did they ever let you have the grenade launcher for it?"

"You know, getting the grant to buy the rifle was easy," Blake grumbled. "But they've been down right stubborn about the grenade launcher."

A Herstal shotgun. Excellent weapon. An M4. Powerful rifle capable of fully automatic fire.

"I think you guys have me outgunned," he commented.

"Fortunately we're all on the same team," Blake responded.

114

"Yeah, fortunate," Hackett said.

When they had unpacked the Jeep and Kelli was satisfied that the horses had been given enough treats, Hackett stood on the porch looking out over the Pines. The women were inside with Baron and Blake. They were making up a grocery list. Blake was going to have one of his deputies go into town and pick up everything they would need. As Betty had been away for several days the list was growing long.

The old house sat at one end of a low ridge. At the other end was a cabin. A plant that looked like some sort of cactus was at the corner of the cabin's front door. Hackett thought it was called a Spanish dagger. He recalled seeing similar plants when he visited his late wife's native New Mexico.

The barn sat on flat ground past and to the left of the cabin. He could see half a dozen horses grazing and playing in the pasture. And one donkey.

Raquel would have loved this place, Hackett thought. Having a place like this was their dream. They had looked at land in New Mexico. They had hoped to move there and build a place like this one when he retired.

Then came the cancer that took her from him. His life ended with hers. He had been dead inside ever since. Dead and angry.

In Anchorage Christopher was busy making calls. He and Anthony Nettleton in Seattle were still trying to get their assigned parties on board with a conference call.

And in Juneau, Monk was frustrated. It now looked like it would be Monday before the summit meeting he had called could take place.

July 22nd

Saturday was an uneventful day in Anchorage and Juneau. The rain for which Southeast was famous fell all day.

The day passed quickly. In the dusk of a rainy Alaska evening, the yacht Integrity was anchored in the remote cove indenting the coastline of Kosciuska Island. A few minutes after nine o'clock a larger ship slipped silently into the cove.

The skippers of the two vessels proceeded through their due diligence routines as they had been instructed. Phone calls were made. Friendly banks accommodated a swift transfer of funds. Crates of sports shoes, designer sunglasses, and perfumes, all counterfeit, were transferred to Integrity and stowed in compartments hidden beneath the false decks. Both vessels were underway in less than three hours.

July 23th

It was almost 80 degrees in Anchorage on Sunday. A very warm day by Southcentral Alaska standards.

Darcey thought it was a good day to get out of the city and find a view other than what they could see from their deck. It didn't take much to convince Christopher and Nancy. The three of them climbed into the black Escalade Darcey had rented.

"You've adapted to Trent's tastes in cars," Christopher said, lightheartedly. "A black SUV."

"Yes, it had to be all black," Darcey said. "When I bring Trent home from the hospital, he will be pleased to be riding in a black vehicle."

Funny, she thought, that she referred to the penthouse as home. Alaska has that effect on people she was discovering.

She recalled a story Robert had told them about that effect. When he was a very young man, he said, he had the good fortune to get to know General Marvin "Muktuk" Marston, a legendary Alaskan who organized the Eskimo Scouts during World War II.

"Alaska is more than a place," the old general told him. "It's a spirit. Some people live here all their lives and never get it. Others step off an airplane and feel it immediately. They're the ones who make Alaska great."

She drove south out of Anchorage on the Seward Highway. Once they passed the bird sanctuary at Potter Marsh it grew quiet in the car. The scenery was spectacular. The Chugach Mountains bordering the road on their left. The waters of Turnagain Arm, a branch of Cook Inlet, splashing to the right. On the far side of the water the mountains of the Kenai Peninsula rose high.

The British explorer Captain James Cook explored the waters around Southcentral Alaska in 1778. He gave his name to the inlet that surrounds Anchorage on two sides. Cook sailed into Alaska waters seeking, as the Europeans had for two centuries before him, the rumored Northwest Passage that would provide a shorter route between Europe, North America, and Asia.

It was said that Cook himself gave Turnagain Arm its name when he realized it was not the legendary Northwest Passage as he had hoped. It was also too shallow to risk proceeding. He ordered his vessels to "Turn again."

They stopped at Bird Point for the view, lingering for photographs. Eventually they arrived in the small community of Girdwood. Technically part of the Municipality of Anchorage, Girdwood was the home of Mount Alyeska, the state's largest ski resort.

It was also home to the Double Musky, a Cajun-influenced restaurant, wildly popular in Alaska, which gained international fame thanks to multiple reviews by influential food critics who had been impressed. Though the restaurant didn't open until five o'clock, Darcey had been told the line formed early so they should arrive by four. Even then, there were at least twenty people already in line when Christopher got out to hold a place for them while Darcey and Nancy went looking for a parking space in the already crowded small lot.

While Darcey, Christopher, and Nancy were enjoying shrimp gumbo and the huge pepper steaks for which the Double Musky was famous, Monk was having a peach martini in Juneau. He had taken a liking to Trent's current favorite cocktail.

It had rained the day before. The sky over Juneau was still gray, which matched Monk's mood. The first martini failed to brighten his outlook. A second, he reasoned, might do the job.

He was frustrated that it had taken so long to arrange the summit meeting he thought critically important. At least it appeared the conference call linking Juneau, Anchorage, Seattle, and San Francisco would take place on Monday. The call would join Trent's troops with the Coast Guard in Juneau and Seattle, the FBI in Anchorage, Seattle and San Francisco, the Anchorage Police Department, and the Alaska State

Troopers Bureau of Investigation. He also included the Juneau and Seattle Police Departments.

The group was larger than he would have liked. Ordinarily he believed the more people involved the better the chance for leaks. In this instance he thought it wise to exclude no one. Monk was confident they had the opportunity to take down one of the most formidable desperados he had ever run into and destroy a major criminal activity. He didn't want someone accidentally stumbling into their operation out of ignorance, giving Segal an opportunity to once again escape in the resulting confusion.

Integrity was en route to the west coast loaded with counterfeit goods. They would be sold for many times what he had paid for them. It was free enterprise at the most basic level. No rules. Business at which only the most ruthless could be successful.

Meanwhile, the yacht Bounty, with its six passengers, was preparing to cruise north to collect a cargo of video games and high-end ladies' accessories, including designer hand bags and shoes. More counterfeit products to flood west coast markets.

Darcey sat by Trent's bed. She had started talking to him when she visited. Dr. Shannon said it was possible he would hear her.

She told him about their evening. The drive along Turnagain Arm. Dinner at the Double Musky. She told him she wanted to bring Kelli back to Anchorage when recovered. Betty and Ivy, too. She wanted to explore more of Alaska.

July 24th

"So that's where that low life got off to," San Francisco's FBI Special Agent in Charge Joseph Brady exploded. "We've been looking for him for four years."

Booth had just told those participating via telephone in Monk's summit meeting that the man known in Alaska as Jim Segal was in reality Pietro Greco, formerly underboss and consigliere in the Rossi Mafia Family.

"You know him, Joseph?" Brady's Seattle counterpart, Charles Cabot, asked.

"Oh yes, Charles, we know him. When the four members of Rossi's criminal alliance imploded, the leader of each group was found murdered. The safe in each office was open and empty as was a safe deposit box belonging to Rossi. And an $8 million yacht owned by one of the gang leaders went missing. So did Greco."

"You think Segal or Greco or whoever was behind all that?" APD Chief Ben Kline asked.

"I think he saw the alliance beginning to crumble and took advantage of the situation," Booth replied. "I always thought he left the Bay area with a lot of money and a new identity. Now we know that's what he did and we know his new identity."

Booth and Nettleton went on to describe the events surrounding Disher's murder and what they had learned about the home port Segal had established on the deserted island in the San Juan group. Monk wrapped it up with his theory that Segal had put together a brilliant scheme to import counterfeit merchandise, using luxury yachts that were as phony as the cargo he imported, the San Juan Island base, and the secluded bays and coves of Southeast Alaska.

From there the discussion moved to strategy. The Coast Guard, Monk noted, was key. Captain Joan Hardie, commander of the combined Seattle-Puget Sound Coast Guard Sector, said she was prepared to commit as many cutters and aircraft as necessary to clear out the nest in the San Juan Islands.

Van Patten volunteered the cutters and support vessels under his command as well as the three Sikorsky Jayhawk helicopters stationed at Sitka. The aircraft could be armed with 7.62 millimeter M240 medium machine guns and Barrett .50 caliber M82 semiautomatic rifles. The cutters could be armed with heavy machine guns and grenade launchers.

Having organized the summit meeting to urge a joint operation, Monk suddenly found himself arguing for restraint.

"We can take the four boats Segal is using for his smuggling operation anytime," he said. "That would give us his cookie jar. Better to maneuver Segal into a position in which we catch him with his hand trapped in the jar. Otherwise he'll only disappear again and show up with another operation somewhere else in the world."

Eventually Monk's view prevailed. All agreed to take a cautious, watchful approach for the time being. The Coast Guard would use its vessels and aircraft to keep tabs on Segal's small fleet of yachts while not appearing overly aggressive.

Coast Guard crews would be instructed to get pictures of the "guests" and crews when they could do so discreetly. Otherwise they were to continue waving friendly greetings to the "wealthy patrons" on deck whenever they encountered one of the yachts. Meanwhile, Captain Hardie's vessels would be watching for traffic to the island Segal had commandeered. They would have to get supplies to the island and their cargo to the mainland.

"They're probably using a variety of vessels," Captain Hardie offered. "We'll spend the next few days observing from afar. When this group decides it's time to act, we might have developed a list of vessels to seize. And once we get inside their home port, there'll be plenty of information leading us to any we miss."

"Joseph and I can take the same approach on land," Cabot said. "We can discreetly watch the comings and goings at the waterfronts in Seattle and San Francisco."

"They might be using secluded coves along your coastline as they're doing in Alaska," Monk suggested.

"Maybe," Brady replied. "But our coastlines down here are a lot more congested. I think they have to be bringing the stuff in right under our noses. They're probably using vessels that seem too obvious to be suspected."

"Sounds to me like we have a plan. But give them no cause for alarm," Monk urged, "until we find a way to drag Segal out into the open."

At the Pines, Hackett had to admit that so far this was the best duty assignment he'd ever been given. He was on the back porch with Jordan Baron and Jack Blake. Baron was expertly flipping burgers on Betty's grill.

"Ivy mixed a little brown sugar into the ground beef," he said. "She says a little sugar makes everything taste better. And I'm grilling up enough burgers to feed you and your men, Jack."

The sheriff sat near the grill, sipping a glass of iced tea.

"The sheriff's department thanks you, Captain Baron," Blake said, saluting the cook with his glass.

Hackett almost felt like he was on vacation. Only the press of the revolver against his hip, and the sight of Jordan's shotgun and Blake's M4 leaning against the wall within easy reach redefined that feeling as sheer buncombe.

The six deputies Blake had on duty around the clock at the Pines were also well armed. Hackett learned the sheriff armed his deputies with Beretta M9s, the same weapon with which the would-be assassins in New Orleans were armed. The only difference was Blake's weapons were the version designed to meet the exacting demands of the U.S. Marine Corps, including a sand resistant magazine. It was known for its low recoil and high degree of accuracy.

Not exactly the same weapon but enough of a similarity to raise a question in Hackett's mind. He recalled Robert Monk's words.

"There is no coincidence in crime, corruption, or politics."

He watched the sheriff and wondered.

In the kitchen, Betty was grilling onions in a black iron skillet. She added a bit of freshly grated nutmeg, a trick she learned from Trent, who was constantly experimenting with spices and ingredients.

Ivy was frying potatoes in duck fat, something she had taught Trent.

"Ain't nothing better than duck fat for making French fries," she told Betty, "I brought some from home because I didn't figure we could find any out here in the country."

Kelli was playing with her baby carriage and a selection of favorite dolls she had brought down from her room. She was in the doorway to the dining room so her grandmothers could keep an eye on her.

That either Betty or Ivy was always close to Kelli was another sign of the seriousness of their situation. It was tense enough that Betty had brought her snake killer, which she usually kept under her bed, into the kitchen. The snake killer was a machete made from a saw blade from her grandfather's lumber mill.

Ivy used a large chef's knife to slice the potatoes. She had taken to walking around the house with the same knife in her hand. She seemed almost disappointed that she hadn't been attacked.

Monk's summit meeting wrapped up in time for him to catch the early afternoon flight to Anchorage. He was back in time to join Darcey, Christopher, and Nancy on the deck for cocktail hour.

Darcey made French 75s for them. She shook gin, simple syrup, and lemon juice over ice before pouring it into chilled martini glasses. She filled each glass about halfway, then topped it off with Mumm's Napa Valley Brut Prestige. It was the cocktail for which Trent was famous made with his favorite wine. He was very much on their minds.

Darcey and Nancy had stuffed some very large Portobello mushrooms for dinner. They removed the stems and finely chopped them. They sautéed the mushroom stems with chopped onion, seasoned with a little salt and pepper. Darcey added what she told Nancy was a secret ingredient for this dish. Cinnamon. Immediately the kitchen was filled with a tantalizing aroma.

When the vegetables were softened, they mixed in thinly sliced deli ham, also chopped into small pieces, and a handful of breadcrumbs. After gently scooping out the gills of the mushrooms, they filled the cavities with the stuffing before laying a slice of cheddar cheese over each one. They would go into the oven for half an hour or so.

As they sipped the cocktails, Darcey pointed out the postage stamp park bordering the waters of Cook Inlet far below the penthouse.

"Wouldn't Kelli have fun in that park?" she asked, rhetorically. "It's so pretty, with the trees and shrubs. And it has all the things she likes to play on when we go to a park."

Darcey still talked to Kelli morning and evening. She visited Trent each evening before bed. Her heart ached with missing both of them. But she wouldn't give up. She would never give up.

Something wasn't right. Segal could feel it. He still had no definitive information on Marshall's fate. He thought he was still alive but didn't know for sure. It was too risky to send someone into the hospital. Segal knew there was a time to take a risk and a time to avoid it. The instinct that allowed him to survive many threatening situations told him now was not the time to take that risk.

It was, however, time to take another risk. One that would be far away from him. It was a step he would rather not take but if Marshall was still alive, he was a formidable enemy. If he was dead, his wife and those around her were equally dangerous.

He recalled the words of the Italian despot, Niccolo Machiavelli.

"Men must either be caressed or else annihilated; they will revenge themselves for small injuries, but cannot do so for great ones; the injury therefore that we do to a man must be such that we need not fear his vengeance."

Marshall and Booth made a mistake when they allowed him to escape the rubble of Rossi's criminal alliance. He wouldn't make the same mistake.

When he received the evening call from Louisiana he would issue orders to take the first step toward annihilation.

Dr. Shannon was still at the hospital when Darcey arrived for her evening visit.

"Any change, Doctor?" Darcey asked.

"Yes and no," was the unexpected response. "Trent is still in a coma but it's not being induced by us now."

"Same question as always," Darcey said. "Is that good or bad?"

"And the same answer. We don't know. He could remain this way indefinitely or he could open his eyes at any time. It's always a wait and see situation."

In her midtown apartment, Jayne Colombo laid awake. The little twit Fiona wasn't responding to her attempt to forge a relationship with her. In the older woman's mind, it was incontrovertible that Fiona intended to replace her at Segal's side.

That would mean the girl must have computer skills. That probably explained what she was doing the night Jayne caught her sneaking out of the office. But her generation was born with a phone in their chubby little hands. And for them, a phone was a computer.

She, too, was considering risk. She decided it was too risky to take Fiona on directly. At least not yet. Better to recruit her own allies. She didn't want to be standing alone when the time came to take on Segal.

That time would come. It would come soon.

July 25th

It was a cool, cloudy day. Most of the guests on board the yacht Bounty were staying inside the main lounge. Two hearty souls, one a middle-aged man whose belly overhung his belt by several inches, the other a young woman who looked as though she'd rather be almost anywhere else, were on deck. They were jigging for halibut. He was enthusiastic. She was not.

They were in Coffman Cove, just north of Ketchikan when the Coast Guard Cutter Bailey Barco spotted them. The skipper slowed his ship as they came abreast of the yacht. He stepped out on deck, a smile on his face, as he waved at the two on the Bounty's aft deck.

"How's the fishing?" the skipper called out.

"Not good," the man said. "We caught a couple of small halibut this morning. Not much after that. Maybe enough for a chowder."

On the yacht's bridge, the vessel's owner inched closer to the closet in which his AR-15 was stowed. He knew Segal's strict orders not to engage with the Coast Guard. He wasn't sure he could stand by and let them take his boat.

"Well, the secret is patience," the friendly skipper advised. He waved again as his ship passed the yacht.

With the skipper distracting them, the two "guests" hadn't noticed the crewman snapping pictures of them. The photos would be e-mailed to the other participants in Monk's summit to see if anyone recognized the pair.

The yacht's owner watched the cutter cruise by with relief. He wouldn't have to decide between disobeying Segal's orders and losing his vessel.

Old man Garth stood on his back porch looking out over Toledo Bend Lake on the Louisiana-Texas border. It was one of the country's largest man-made lakes created by damning the Sabine River. The project was jointly funded by the states of Louisiana and Texas. No federal money involved. That wouldn't happen these days when the states looked to the feds for everything.

He was dressed in his usual bib overalls with no shirt. He didn't especially like the bib overalls but with his big belly they were comfortable. He was wearing work boots, which he hadn't bothered to lace. He didn't like boots to be tight on his feet.

Garth was over eighty now. The thin wisps of hair on his head were snow white. The doctor in town had warned him about being so over weight. He had said Garth's heart would go out one of the days. He couldn't expect it to continue pumping blood through that oversized body forever.

The old man didn't worry much about that. He figured he'd die when his time came and not before. He didn't worry about much of anything.

He left the family farm before he turned twenty. He always hated that farm. He kept it after he inherited it but only because it was convenient for hiding stolen merchandise.

Once the dam was built his goal was to have a house on the lake. A nice house. And he got it, too. One of the first ones built on the water. One of the nicest. The owner hadn't wanted to sell, especially at the low ball price Garth offered. He changed his mind after Garth's oldest boy, Stuart, broke only one of his arms. That and Garth's threat to turn the man's wife over to all three of his boys. The man took Garth's offer and quickly left the parish without talking to the sheriff.

Garth chuckled when he thought of Sheriff Jack Blake. Old Jack had been trying to bust him for years but never could pin anything on him.

Not that there was nothing to pin on him. The truth was that Garth never worked a day in his life. He figured out early on he had no need to work when he was so good at stealing stuff from the folks who did. Most of the time he got away clean. Occasionally he had to send his sons to "reason" with one of his victims.

This morning he was thinking about the phone call he had received the night before. The man needed a job done. A mutual friend suggested he call Garth.

The job seemed simple enough. Shoot a place up a little. The kind of thing Garth and his sons were good at. And the guy was willing to make a generous deposit in Garth's bank to pay for the family's time.

He was going to have to round up three other men to help with this job. Garth didn't like that. He preferred to use only his sons. Family could be trusted. Outsiders were always a risk. But the man with the money was paying generously. Enough to make the risk worthwhile.

"Stuart," the old man called loudly. "Come up here, son, and bring your brothers, Sterling and Mackie. We got work to do."

In Anchorage, Jayne Colombo sat at her desk in the office of JS Bistro. Segal hadn't yet arrived. She was looking over a job application filled out by one of the kitchen workers.

Segal had made the decisions on hiring the chef and Maitre d' but left her to hire all the other employees. She had generally hired reliable workers. One she hired for other reasons.

Dennis Caine had been arrested more than once, always for violent crimes. Assault with a deadly weapon. Attempted murder. He had done a little time but most of the cases ended in the charges being dismissed for lack of evidence. She suspected there were other crimes for which he was never charged. From what she knew of him, he had lived, in the words of the song, la vida loca. The crazy life.

She went downstairs to the kitchen where Caine was working. He had a face that was handsome in an unfriendly way, a look she found enticing. He was always rumpled, his brown hair uncombed, his face sporting a two-day beard. She really didn't care what he looked like as long as he did what he was told.

Jayne walked through the kitchen, appearing to be doing nothing but observing. She paused when she came to Caine's station. He was slicing cheese. She watched him handle the knife deftly.

Stepping closer to him, she spoke softly.

"I might have some extra work for you if you're interested," she said.

He continued slicing cheese without looking up.

"What kind of work?"

"The kind we don't want to discuss here," she said. She knew his shift ended at six o'clock. She told him to meet her at a Spenard bar at eight. Spenard was the old section of midtown Anchorage. It was where her apartment was located.

Only a barely noticeable nod of his head indicated his agreement.

Segal was in an extraordinarily good mood when he arrived at the restaurant shortly before noon.

Stopping by the kitchen on his way to the office, he sought out Fiona. "Are you ready for Juneau? Ready for an adventure?" he asked, cheerfully.

"Right now? Today?" she asked, trying to sound like an innocent girl.

Segal was amused at what he took for naiveté.

"No, not today. Tomorrow. I've booked us on the midday flight. We'll take off shortly after eleven o'clock and be in Juneau before one. We'll be there for five days, maybe a week, so pack accordingly."

When Segal walked away, Fiona let out a deep breath. Events were moving quickly. She felt her heart racing. Not from fear. No, not fear. Anticipation.

The rain had cooled the city. It felt more like an evening for a fireplace rather than the deck. They left the door to the deck open. The sound of the drizzling rain was comforting. They stayed inside for cocktails.

Monk was in charge of the fireplace. By the time Darcey and Nancy had mixed rum and cokes for everyone, there was a comfortable blaze taking the damp chill from the air.

Darcey stood looking out the window at the view to the east. The city of Anchorage with its scattering of tall buildings set before the backdrop of the Chugach Mountains. She wondered what it would look like in winter. When the city was wrapped in a white blanket of snow.

Caine was sitting at the bar when Jayne walked in. She told him to get her a scotch and join her at a table away from listening ears.

Sipping the strong liquor, she questioned Caine. She had to find out what he was willing to do. How far he was willing to go. It didn't take her long to decide he had no limits. She decided he was kinky as was she.

Could she depend on him? Her instinct told her she could. At least enough for one job. There would be only one. After that she wouldn't need him.

She asked him if he had any friends who could be trusted. Friends who would do what they were told. Friends who also had little in the way of limits.

"Yeah, I got a couple," Caine said. "Brooke and J.B. We done a few jobs together."

"Brooke? A woman?"

"Sort of," Caine said, disparagingly. "She's meaner than J.B. I'd trust her over him to get a job done. But he's ok."

After an hour and a second scotch, Jayne was warming to the thought of working with Caine and, from his brief description, his friend, Brooke. She felt the old itch inside. She and Caine and maybe Brooke might have some fun together. She would have to kill them anyway once they did the job for her.

Darcey sat by Trent's bed at the hospital.

"What would you say to a white Christmas?" she asked him. His eyes remained closed. He didn't speak.

"You didn't say no," she said out loud, a smile on her face.

It didn't trouble her to talk about Christmas. Trent would be with them. She wouldn't think of it any other way.

JS Bistro was closed. All the customers and employees were gone.

All but one.

Fiona was busy in the upstairs office. It was her second nocturnal visit to the office. The first time had been to reconnoiter. To learn what operating system and software were installed on Colombo's computer. The purpose of this visit was to get into that computer. She worked quickly and efficiently. It didn't take long for her to accomplish her goal.

July 26th

"Is there a hat maker in Anchorage? Or a store that carries men's hats?" Darcey asked Robert.

"Yes, there is a store that carries Stetsons and other name brands. At least there used to be. Haven't been there in years. I'll check to see if it's still in business or if it's been driven out by the big box stores. Do you need a hat?"

"Not for me," she said. "For Trent. He's going to come out of the hospital soon. And he'll have a bandage on his head. I want to get him a hat he'll love and want to wear to save him the embarrassment of being seen with his head wrapped in gauze. He won't want people to see him all bandaged up."

"What kind of hat?" Robert asked.

"A Stetson if you can find one. Pinched front. Western style with the front of the brim turned down and a slight upward curl on the sides."

"I'll see what I can do."

"And Robert, it should be black," Darcey said.

"Of course. It's for Trent. It couldn't be any other color," the old friend said.

Segal and Fiona landed in the rain not long after noon. Cameron McGraw met them and drove directly to the building that would soon house JS Bistro Southeast with its apartment, which doubled as living quarters and office, on the second floor.

There were two bedrooms in the apartment. Segal had instructed McGraw to clear his bedroom for Fiona. He should plan to sleep on the couch, Segal directed.

He didn't want to complete his seduction of the young woman until he got her alone on the boat. That seemed the proper time for the next phase of what he viewed as their nascent relationship. A very exciting next phase.

Fiona put her small bag in what was usually McGraw's bedroom. Segal tossed his bag into his own room. He left few clothes in Juneau simply because he didn't want to be bothered doing laundry when he was in the state's capital city.

McGraw led the way downstairs into the restaurant. While Segal was unhappy with McGraw for being slow to let him know what he found out about Monk, he was pleased with the appearance of the restaurant. The front of the house was in place. Tables, chairs, and decoration all completed and in place. It looked ready for customers. It looked like it would attract customers.

The kitchen was almost done. There was still some work to do to get the walk-in freezer going properly. Fiona proved herself helpful by pointing out how the prep stations could be rearranged slightly to make the work flow smoothly and more efficiently.

Segal was impressed with the young woman's intelligence. He had no intention of a entering into a long term relationship with her. But perhaps he could dump her without firing her. She could be an asset. If not, she was replaceable.

It was another cool, wet evening in Anchorage. Robert again got a blaze going in the main parlor's fireplace while Darcey mixed Trent's peach martinis for everyone.

She went out on the deck with her cocktail. For long minutes she stood staring out over Cook Inlet. The clouds were blocking most of the Alaska Range in the distance. She could see Fire Island with its wind farm, the large blades turning slowly. Muktuk Marston's thoughts on what it meant to be an Alaskan were on her mind.

Later that night Jayne knocked on the door of Dennis Caine's apartment in Fairview on the east side of downtown. Caine's friends, Brooke and J.B., were there to meet her. More importantly they were there for her assessment.

Brooke and J.B. were there. Each of the three had a beer. Caine offered her one. She wasn't a beer drinker but accepted to put them at ease.

The apartment was about what Jayne would have expected. Dirty dishes in the sink. Garbage can overflowing. Through the door of one bedroom she could see a rumpled, unmade bed and clothes on the floor. She didn't live there. She didn't care about such things.

The door to what was probably a second bedroom was closed. That meant one of the three slept on the couch. Probably J.B.

Brooke was younger than Jayne expected. She had brown hair which she wore up in a bun. She would have been pretty had it not been for the mean look of her eyes. Jayne imagined she had destroyed many a would-be lover.

J.B. was a small, older man, face smoothly shaved and gray hair with a bald spot on the back of his head. He was dressed in a coat and tie. He wore an unwavering smile. The mark of the professional confidence man. But his mouth was small. The smile looked more painful than pleasant. Jayne didn't know what the J.B. stood for and didn't ask. She didn't care. They weren't going to be friends.

The only thing she wanted from the three of them was that they obey her order to kill. Who and when were her decisions.

July 29th

Segal, McGraw, and Fiona spent the next two days working in the new restaurant. McGraw and Fiona got their hands dirty. Segal not so much. His manager and the young woman worked well together. They seemed comfortable with each other from the moment they met.

Segal saw no reason to become involved in the actual work of preparing a restaurant for opening. As the man putting up the money, he was entitled to remain management only.

He was pleased with the progress. He thought they would be ready to take delivery on provisions by next week. The employees McGraw had already hired would be on site then. The restaurant could be ready to open by the following week. McGraw had already done some preliminary advertising. Segal told him to pick a day for the opening and start promoting it.

He had planned to take Fiona out on the boat for the weekend. But the forecast for Saturday was for rain. The long range forecast showed sunshine and seventy on the following Tuesday. That would be the day. It would be beautiful on the water. He would keep her busy in the restaurant until then.

Meanwhile, Bounty was due to meet the supplier on Saturday night to pick up a cargo of video games and ladies' high-end accessories, including hand bags and shoes. Segal had no intention of being in the neighborhood when the transfer took place.

On Sunday evening, the beautiful 1920s yacht Justice would pull away from the dock in the San Juans, its bow pointed north. It was scheduled to take on a load of pharmaceuticals. Lipitor. Prednisone. Xanax. All counterfeit. Segal's favorite cargo. So small and lightweight the small vessels could easily pack boxes worth millions.

It was true that there were some whose high cholesterol, lung diseases, and anxiety attacks would worsen when they took what they thought was legitimate medication. But that was the chance they took when they paid low prices from a source other than a pharmacy.

Segal always hoped Justice had no problems. It was a beautiful yacht. When he could find a replacement vessel for her, he intended to buy it. If the owner didn't want to sell, he knew ways to convince her.

Every day a Coast Guard vessel or aircraft made some contact with one of Segal's fleet of four yachts. Some days an aircraft flew over the San Juan Islands snapping pictures of the deserted island Segal had taken over. Other days might find a chopper from the base at Sitka flying by a yacht, far enough away to avoid suspicion but close enough to snap more pictures.

And there was the occasional day when a cutter or buoy tender passed by. Those events were always accompanied by friendly waves and smiles from the Coast Guard crews. Even the occasional wolf whistle if an attractive guest was on deck.

The first photographs of the two guests fishing from the deck of Bounty resulted in only one hit. No one recognized the man. But Captain Nettleton reported that the woman was known to the Seattle police.

"She's Jeanne Conrad," he said. "At least that's the name she goes by. We've busted her a few times for prostitution and possession. She's definitely not wealthy and I would be very surprised if any rich man would take her along on a vacation, unless he wanted to live dangerously."

In Anchorage, temperatures were rising. It was forecast to be in the seventies again by the beginning of the week. They had returned to the deck for cocktail hour.

For a change of pace, Darcey made Mint Juleps, the old southern favorite. It was nothing but bourbon, simple syrup, and muddled mint leaves, with a few whole leaves for garnish. It was also why in the old days little old ladies sat on the front porch in the late afternoons, giggling like school girls.

Robert had brought the hat Darcey requested. She held it now, admiring it. Beaver felt, black, pinched front crown, brim turned slightly down in front, gently curled on the sides.

"It's perfect, Robert," she said. "Thanks."

She and Nancy had experimented in the kitchen by creating a korma, a spicy Indian stew with heavy curry. Their version was vegetables only. Cauliflower, potatoes, and green beans. They added a little something of their own creation. A pureed mango. And hot pepper. Very hot pepper. To offset the heat, they created a traditional Indian raita. A cool yogurt and cucumber sauce.

Robert was a confirmed carnivore. The thought of a vegetarian dinner wasn't appealing. But he would be polite.

Christopher was known to eat most anything that didn't try to eat him first. Maybe even a few of those.

Same day. Dimension unknown.

Trent was tired. His plane of existence remained an enigma. He felt suspended somewhere between life and death. An existential enigma.

It was time.

He couldn't open his eyes. He couldn't open his mouth to speak.

But he spoke.

He spoke to God. A private conversation. A personal conversation.

"I don't know your plan for me, God. But I'm ready. I'm tired. If it's time for me to go, I won't resist. If it's not time for me to go, I'm prepared for that as well. This isn't for me to decide. This is for a power far greater than am I."

He lay quietly for some minutes.

Beginning with his feet, his toes, he felt a tingling sensation. Much like the sensation when the circulation is cut off in an arm and the blood comes rushing back when the arm is released.

At first it wasn't unpleasant. It began to move slowly from his feet across his ankles and up his calves.

The sensation began to intensify as it moved inexorably up his thighs. It crossed over his pelvis and moved into his lower midsection.

As it moved into his chest and upper back it became uncomfortable. Thousands, millions of tiny pinpricks covering every inch of his skin. Unrelenting. Constantly stinging his flesh.

As it moved up his neck Trent wanted to scream. He could not.

The pinpricks reached his chin, crossed his lips, his nose, his cheeks. It moved over his eyes, over his forehead, covered his scalp.

It felt as though he had been dropped into a mound of fire ants. Every cell was stinging.

He could stand no more.

Suddenly his eyes popped open. He sat up. He tried to scream but no sound came out.

The tingling pinpricks stopped. Trent fell back onto the bed.

The last sight appearing to him before he lapsed into darkness was a couple watching him from across the room. A man and a woman. His mother and father. Slowly they faded away. They were holding hands.

There was forgiveness.

There was peace.

Dimension unnerving.

August 1ˢᵗ

The sun was peaking from behind the clouds on Tuesday morning when Segal piloted the Sea Ray Sundancer 350 slowly from Juneau's Aurora Basin small boat harbor. It would reach seventy degrees today. A perfect day on the waters of Southeast Alaska. The forecast called for gradual warming throughout the week.

Segal had waited for this day. He had no intention of rushing it. It was an experience he would relish. It would be memorable. He didn't care if Fiona enjoyed it as much as he would. He had no plans to eliminate her when he was done with her. When he tired of her, he would simply give her some money and send her away. Or keep her as an employee if she was adult enough to accept the job. And if he thought he could trust her when his back was turned. That would be a judgment call for another day.

Today they would cruise south down Gastineau Channel and circle Douglas Island. He planned to turn north toward Glacier Bay. He expected her to be overwhelmed by the scenery. The towering mountains running straight to sky from ocean. The fjords separating myriad small islands.

That evening he would prepare steaks for them, which they would eat either on deck or in the main cabin, as weather dictated. It would be pleasant but not the setting for the main event.

The following evening they would arrive at Chicagof Island for dinner at the Clove Hitch Café. The restaurant had instructions for preparing the food he had personally selected and had sent to them from Juneau. There would be wine at dinner. More on the boat. He had laid in a selection of very expensive bottles.

There was no way Fiona could resist the seduction, which she surely expected.

To cap this day, he had received word that his plan for the group gathered at the Pines would be carried out that night.

He leaned back in the captain's chair on the small bridge of the Sundancer. Behind and below him, Fiona had taken off her jacket. She wore a light top and again the form-fitting jeans. She was stretched out on the padded bench, enjoying the sun warming the open deck.

He was unrepentant in his anticipation of what he had planned for the young beauty.

Darcey sat by Trent's bed that evening. She talked to him about the day, which had been more boring than anything else. She told him she would be glad when he was back. She had made margaritas for cocktail hour.

"I just can't get the hang of those things," she was saying. "You make them so much better."

Trent's eyes opened. He looked at her.

For a moment it didn't register with her that his eyes were open. And then it did.

"Oh, Trent! You're awake! You're back!"

He tried to speak. He could open his mouth but no sound came out. His hand moved weakly to this throat. It didn't help. It was the first time he felt real fear. Would he never talk again? Had they, for some reason, removed his larynx? For the first time since he was a boy, Trent felt panic approaching.

She wrapped her arms around him. She kissed him. This time he could feel her lips. He tried to smile and almost made it.

"Oh, wait. I have to find Doctor Shannon."

Darcey ran to the nurse's station just outside the door of Trent's room.

"Is Doctor Shannon still in the hospital?"

"Yes, Ma'am."

"Please tell her that my husband is awake."

Having said that, Darcey ran back to Trent's side.

She was holding Trent's hand when Doctor Shannon entered the room.

"So you decided you were ready to join us, Mr. Marshall," the doctor said in her best bedside manner.

Trent tried to speak again. This time he managed something between a grunt and a croak. Again his hand went to his throat, his eyes questioning.

"You've been in a coma for more than three weeks, Mr. Marshall," the doctor explained, as she reviewed his charts and checked the various machines monitoring Trent's life functions. "You've been on constant oxygen during that time. It dries everything out. You can talk as soon as you get some moisture over your vocal chords."

"It's probably a blessing that he can't talk this evening," Darcey said, happily. "He'd be telling us to let him out of here."

Dr. Shannon laughed.

"Well, this is a big first step. We'll be sending him home soon enough, assuming there are no setbacks."

It was midnight at the Pines.

Three cars were gathered on a dirt road on the far side of the pasture, out of sight of the both the house and the highway. Five men were listening to Stuart, the oldest of the Garth brothers, as he gave them final instructions.

"Sterling, you take Roy up to that abandoned warehouse. Leave the car there and sneak up behind the house through the woods. Mackie, you and Joe are the smallest. You two crawl across the pasture to the barn and go up toward the house that way. Ya'll got it?"

The five men gathered around Stuart all mumbled their responses.

"Blake's deputies have the driveway entrance blocked with one of their vehicles. Race and I will ram into it with this old pickup truck. We'll keep them occupied while y'all move in. And remember, we want lots of noise. Fire your rifles. Shout. Make any kind of noise you can. We'll give y'all ten minutes to get into position before we hit the driveway."

Hackett awoke in the middle of the night as usual. He pulled on his pants and a shirt, slipping his feet into shoes, not bothering with socks. He slid the Korth Sky Marshal into its holster on his hip.

He wandered through the house. Kelli was sleeping soundly with Betty. Ivy and Jordan were both asleep in the bedrooms to which they had been assigned.

He went downstairs and stepped out onto the porch. It was still in the seventies. The moon moved in and out of sight as clouds sailed across the night sky.

Hackett knew the sheriff had six deputies on duty around the clock. Two were with the car blocking entry into the drive leading up to the big house. A second car was concealed in the barn. The two deputies there stayed out of sight, watching the pasture and the woods to the right through the barn windows.

He knew a third car was parked somewhere on the far side of the woods bordering the rear of the house. He thought there might be a building of some kind over there. But he hadn't had an opportunity to see for himself.

He heard a horse snort. Then another. Raquel grew up with horses in New Mexico. He remembered her telling him that when a horse snorted rather than neighed it was a sign of danger. He saw the horses shying away from something. Looking closer he saw two figures. Men crawling across the pasture. He turned to go back inside.

Stuart's watch said it had been exactly ten minutes. Race was behind the wheel of the stolen pickup truck. Stuart worked the lever action of his rifle and told Race to floorboard it.

With the headlights off, they were stopped on the highway around a bend and perhaps two hundred yards from the drive into the Pines. With Stuart's order, Race threw the truck into gear and shoved the accelerator to the floor. The wheels spun briefly, then caught and sent the old truck escalating down the highway.

Reaching the entry into the drive, Race whirled the wheel, sending the truck crashing into the SUV with the sheriff's decal on the door.

Hackett was climbing the stairs when he heard the sound of vehicle hitting vehicle, followed immediately by shots fired. The first shots sounded like they came from a rifle, firing slowly. Rifles that had to be cocked for each shot. Bolt or maybe even lever action. Return fire was from smaller weapons, firing rapidly. Semiautomatics. The Berettas with which the deputies were armed.

Hackett was already at the door to Betty's bedroom when Jordan came running out of his room. He was working the action of his shotgun to chamber one shell from the five round magazine and loading a sixth.

"Get the women together," he shouted as he ran downstairs wearing only pants. No shirt. No shoes. Pulling his phone from his pocket as he ran down the stairs, he pushed the speed dial for Jack Blake.

"Jack, we're under attack," he shouted when the sheriff answered. Saying nothing else, he ended the call and thrust the phone back into his pocket.

Hackett watched the younger cop run down the stairs and out the front door. He wasn't young any more. He was old now. Too old.

He knocked on Ivy's door, then opened it.

"Join us in Betty's room, Ivy," he directed. "I need you all together."

She was already up, pulling on a robe, and reaching for the large chef's knife, which had become her constant companion. When they got to Betty's room, they found Kelli clinging to her grandmother. Betty had one arm around the child, her snake killer, the machete, in her other hand.

The gunshots had awakened everyone. The little girl was frightened. The women were frightened.

Hackett didn't have the option to be frightened. He had a job to do.

He stood by the door, the small, deadly Korth Sky Marshal in his hand.

Outside a deadly war was being waged. Baron flattened himself on the floor of the porch, presenting a small target as he assessed the situation.

A large pickup, probably a dually, had crashed into the side of the SUV blocking entrance to the Pines. He could see the deputies crouched behind their ruined vehicle, returning fire. He could barely make out two dim figures firing rifles from behind the bed of the truck.

Jordan could also hear gunfire from the thicket behind the house. For the moment, he could only hope the deputies stationed back there were holding their own.

At the head of the driveway, one of the attackers attempted to rush the deputies. The man ran toward them, firing his rifle. He didn't get far. A nine millimeter round from one of the Berettas struck him in the lower leg, which collapsed beneath him. Jordan thought the bullet broke either the man's tibia or fibula. Either way, he was effectively out of action.

His partner was temporarily more fortunate. One of his carefully placed shots hit a defending deputy in the right hand. It was likely not a serious wound but it caused him to drop his weapon.

Using the muzzle flash of the shot that wounded his partner as a target, the second deputy fired three rounds at the attacker. From his vantage point, Jordan could see the man dropping his rifle, his hand going to his neck as he collapsed. It could have been a killing shot. At worst it was crippling.

Satisfied that the two men guarding the entrance had effectively halted the attack from that direction, Jason turned his attention to the gunfire now coming from the direction of the barn. The two assassins who crawled across the pasture had leaped to their feet, firing their rifles as they ran toward it.

One veered toward the cabin at the far end of the ridge. A deputy fired four times, missing all four. His target made it to the cover of the cabin.

The assassin's companion wasn't as lucky. Still charging the barn, thinking to give his partner cover, he was stopped by the second deputy, who fired twice. The running man's left leg collapsed, one of the deputy's bullets plowing through a thick thigh dropping him to the ground.

With the deputies in the barn taking the wounded assailant into custody, Jordan turned his attention back to the man who had ducked behind the cabin. The rifle the assailant carried had greater range than Jordan's shotgun.

At the cabin, Mackie Garth pressed himself against the wall of the old building. He saw his companion fall at the edge of the barn. Both deputies were busy with the wounded man. Since Mackie had disappeared into the darkness, the deputies weren't focused on him. He waited.

On the porch of the main house, Jordan lay still. Also waiting. He needed the man to get within fifty yards. Jordan was patient. His opponent less so. Within two minutes, Jordan saw a dark figure come from behind the cabin, crouching, making his way slowly to the house.

Mackie Garth thought he was in the clear. He didn't see Jordan waiting for him in the dark. Confident he faced no opposition in his run to the house, the man raised to his full height, thinking to reach the house unopposed.

To his surprise, Jordan rose to a kneeling position. Mackie hastily fired his rifle from the waist while he ran, managing to miss the entire house. Jordan fired the Herstal twelve gauge twice. Eighteen balls of lead powered by the additional powder of a magnum load struck Mackie square in the stomach, almost cutting him in half. He dropped to the ground, dead before his face touched grass.

The New Orleans detective started to stand but a bullet whizzing by his ear caused him to drop to his belly again. Looking back at the heavy thicket of trees to the rear of the house he saw a fifth man charging toward him, firing a lever action rifle as he ran.

Jordan crawled over to the corner of the house, waiting again for the man to come within the fifty yard effective range of the shotgun. He needn't have bothered.

From near the conjoined truck and car at the front of the drive came a series of three round bursts from an automatic weapon. A frightening sound, which brought the rifleman up short.

"Drop your weapon and get on your belly," came the roar from Sheriff Jack Blake, "unless you want to try your luck with that saddle gun against my M4. Let me give you a clue. You'll lose!"

Sterling Garth didn't need additional information. He tossed the rifle away, held up his hands, and fell flat onto the ground.

Jordan listened for a few seconds but heard no more shots coming from behind the thicket. He stood up and walked toward Blake, shotgun still at the ready.

"About time you got here," Jordan said. "Your men and I about had the mess all cleared up."

"Where's Hackett?" the sheriff asked.

"I told him to stay with Kelli and the women. Didn't want them to be alone in case some of those guys made it past us. I'll go check on him now."

"I'll see what the damage out here is," Blake said. "I've already called for as many ambulances as we can get. They should start arriving any minute."

The sheriff tossed a lever action rifle onto the porch.

"Looks like a knock off of an 1866 Yellowboy Trapper," he said. ".45 long colt. It was an improvement on the Henry repeating rifle and forerunner of the 1873 Winchester that became so popular."

"Why would they use rifles like this? Seems like they would have wanted something at least semiautomatic," Jordan asked, puzzled.

"Somebody hired country boys for this job. A lot of people around here favor this type of rifle. I had a deputy who carried one in her car because she couldn't hit the barn with a handgun."

Upstairs in Betty's room, Hackett heard the front door open. He was facing the women, his snubnosed revolver in his hand, cocked, when Jordan announced himself.

Jordan was surprised at the way Hackett had positioned himself but said nothing.

"It's all over," he said. "You can put that thing away."

Hackett nodded, releasing the hammer gently and sliding the small weapon into its holster.

"One of my men guarding the drive took a shot to the hand," Blake reported when Baron and Hackett joined him on the porch. "Not serious. Enough to get him a few weeks off and a commendation. Both my guys in the barn are ok. But one of the guys at the old warehouse took a serious shot to the head. He's still alive. Hope he makes it. He's a good man."

"What about our visitors?" Jordan asked.

"Oh, them," Blake snorted. "They didn't fare so well. The two who hit the front are in bad shape. One got a leg shattered. He won't ever walk normally again. The man with him was shot in the neck. Serious wound. He's alive but in bad shape."

"I took out one of the guys who came through the pasture," Jordan said. "He's over there, between the house and the cabin. I don't doubt he's dead. He took two twelve gauge double aught buck magnums to the belly."

"Yeah, he's gone. Painful way to go. One of my guys in the barn put a bullet through the other one's thigh," the sheriff reported.

"The shooter who came through the woods gave up, didn't he?" Jordan pointed out.

"Yeah, Sterling Garth," Jack said. "The dead man is his younger brother, Mackie. The oldest Garth boy, Stuart, led the assault. Sterling was smart enough to figure out a lever action rifle was no match for a fully automatic M4. He took the diplomatic way out and surrendered. Over at the old warehouse behind the trees his partner was hit in a knee, another one who'll be limping."

Hackett listened. He said nothing.

Blake, Baron, and Hackett left the care of the wounded to the arriving EMTs and ambulances. The dead man was quickly and quietly enclosed in a body bag and spirited away. Blake's deputies took the assailants into custody as their wounds were tended.

The three men went upstairs to Betty's room where Kelli was being comforted by her grandmothers.

"Are the bad men gone, Sheriff Jack?" she asked, in her trembling, little girl voice.

"Yes, sweetheart, they're gone," Blake said kindly. "They won't ever bother you again."

He sat on the edge of the bed. Kelli immediately threw herself on him, her little arms going around his neck. He held her, comforting her.

"You're safe, sweetheart. I promise you are."

August 2nd

It was a rainy day in Anchorage. But the rain dampened no one's mood.

The day started with the alarming call from Jordan Baron in which he reported the attack on the Pines. Darcey's fright quickly turned to relief. She was comforted more when Jack Blake got on the phone to assure her the protectors of her family had broken completely their enemy's ability to launch future attacks.

Now Darcey was in Trent's hospital room, accompanied for the first time by Christopher, Nancy, and Robert. Trent was still very weak. He was speaking now though his voice was low and scratchy.

He was sitting up and sporting his new black hat. Darcey's request to Robert to find the hat was a good call. She knew her husband well. He was a good man but his pride would never allow him to appear in public with his head wrapped in gauze. A black hat was another story entirely.

Robert and Christopher had brought Trent up to date on all they had learned and everything that had happened.

"So, Robert, is this nightmare over?" Trent croaked.

"It's over for the ladies in Louisiana," Robert replied. "Whoever Segal found to attack the Pines won't try it again. He can't even if he wants to. They lost all six soldiers sent to do the job. Worse for them, all but one are still alive. One surrendered without firing a shot. Some of them will talk to save themselves as best they can."

"Do you think they can lay a trail to Greco's door?" Trent remembered the former Mafioso from San Francisco.

"I don't know yet," Robert said. "But we're not going let up on Mr. Greco, or Segal, or whatever he wants to call himself. I do think James and Jordan can return home. Sheriff Blake and his crew have proved themselves perfectly capable of protecting the Pines."

147

"But let's not make the mistake of thinking the danger is over up here," Christopher added.

"I agree," Robert said. "Segal is still on the loose and we don't know where. He flew to Juneau last week and spent a few days working on his restaurant. He had a young woman with him. Yesterday he was seen leaving the harbor on his boat. The young woman was on board. He's somewhere on the water in Southeast now."

Segal was riding at anchor in a small cove near the shore of Chichagof Island. He had been in a rage since he received a phone call a few minutes earlier. Fiona was staying away from him as much as possible on a thirty-five foot boat.

The phone call was from his contact in Louisiana, reporting on the disastrous attempt to storm the farm where Marshall's family had taken refuge. Segal at times screamed into the phone. Fiona couldn't help but overhear his side of the conversation.

"Do I have nothing but fools working for me?" he shouted at one point. "I didn't tell you to launch a full-scale attack on the farm. One of your men is dead, four others wounded, and one surrendered without firing a shot. Your men shot two cops. Two! Do you know what happens when you shoot a cop? All of you involved in this disaster better get as far away from that place as you can. Cops don't give up when they're after somebody who shot one of their own. Those men shot two! And you can bet they'll give you up to save themselves."

Fiona knew the original plan had been for the two of them to have a special dinner at a seaside café near where they were anchored. She knew Segal had gone to a lot of trouble to set up what he thought would be a romantic evening ending with more wine on the boat and, no doubt, with the two of them together in the large bed in the bow cabin.

Fiona had her own plan. It was now midafternoon. There were several hours of daylight remaining. She had made a phone call herself earlier in the day. Now she occasionally glanced at the sky.

Her phone was set on silent. She felt the vibration and read the text. It was time to put her plan into action. She went inside the boat's cabin and to the small bar. Opening a bottle of sparkling wine and retrieving a container of orange juice from the small refrigerator, she quickly made two mimosas.

Segal ended the call and tossed the phone across the deck. He was staring out to sea. Furious. Everything he had built was now threatened because of the incompetence of those fools in Louisiana. Fiona picked up his phone and slipped it into her pocket.

In the distance a single engine airplane on floats was flying through the clear Southeast sky. Segal paid no attention. It was a common sight.

"You need to relax, Mr. Segal," Fiona cooed, handing him the champagne flute.

He felt himself relax a little as he accepted the drink from the smiling, sexy young woman. At least his plan for her seemed to be working.

"That's very thoughtful of you, Fiona," he said as he took a sip. "It's nice to have at least one person around me who can think."

He put his arm around her and leaned to kiss her. She diplomatically avoided the contact by clinking her glass to his.

"Salute, Pietro!" she said, offering the traditional Italian toast, as she drained her glass.

"Salute," Segal replied, finishing his own cocktail.

Something suddenly didn't seem right. What was it? Did she say "Salute!"? He hadn't heard anyone say that since Don Rossi died. Did she call him Pietro? He hadn't been called Pietro since the day he killed Don Rossi.

He felt suddenly drowsy.

"You put something in my drink," he accused her.

"How clever of you to figure that out," she said, with a sneer, "and so quickly."

The small aircraft was coming closer.

"What...what..." he stammered, struggling to keep his eyes open.

"Oh, just a little Rohypnol. Actually quite a lot of Rohypnol. You're going to take a little nap," she said, "though I can't promise you'll feel better when you awaken."

Segal tried to stand but couldn't hold his balance. He tumbled to the deck.

The last thing he saw was the girl pulling the red and black striped wig from her head and shaking loose her dark brown natural hair.

The last sounds he heard were the laughter of the girl and an airplane engine.

The young woman left Pietro Greco to lie where he fell as she watched the Cessna 185 touch down gently on the water. The pilot cut the single engine and let the craft's momentum carry it on toward the boat.

149

The door on the pilot's side opened. Cameron McGraw climbed out to stand on the pontoon. The woman tossed him a line that she had already tied off on one of the boat's stern cleats. The pilot tied the other end to a strut on the port pontoon before leaping onto the deck.

The young woman put his arms around his neck, hugging him. He kissed her cheek.

"How's my favorite niece?" he asked.

She looked down at Greco lying on the deck.

"Doing fine, Uncle Jess," she said. "Just fine."

Dr. Shannon shooed Trent's visitors away after two hours.

"He's still weak," she told them. "We have to be careful not to wear him out. At the rate he's improving, it won't be long before you have him home."

Back at the penthouse, Robert opened two bottles of Mumm's Napa Brut Prestige, Trent's favorite wine. Gathered in the large family room, with a comfortable blaze in the fireplace, they toasted the survival of their recovering friend.

Darcey had found some huge artichokes at one of the farmers' markets scattered around the city. She served them with either mayonnaise or melted butter, or a combination of both.

It felt like the most peaceful evening they had enjoyed in a long time. They weren't so foolish as to think it would last.

The man known in Alaska as Jim Segal awoke screaming in pain. He was lying on a bench in the boat's cabin. He was alone. His arms were spread-eagled, hands tied to bolts that had been screwed into the bulkhead behind him.

The unbearable pain came from his right hand. The hand missing its forefinger. A rough bandage had been applied to stop the bleeding.

Someone entered the cabin. Segal was surprised to see a woman who looked like Fiona but with dark brown hair. The black and red hair was a wig now lying on the boat's small dining table. Lying next to a twenty-four inch bolt cutter and a finger. His finger! He moaned in shock. In pain.

Then reality veered completely out of control when Cameron McGraw stepped into the cabin.

"McGraw!" Greco cried out. "What are you doing here? Untie me!" McGraw smiled.

"His name's not McGraw, Pietro," the young woman said. "His name is Jess Bell. He's my uncle. My mother's brother."

"What's that got to do with me? He was recommended to me!"

"Looks like you don't have as many friends as you thought, Pietro," the woman said.

"And why do you keep calling me Pietro? My name is Jim. Jim Segal."

"You don't recognize me, do you, Pietro?" the young woman said, obviously amused. She had dreamed about this moment for so long it was almost as though she was repeating a memorized speech. But there was far too much emotion attached for it to be a rote performance."

"I never saw you before you showed up at my restaurant looking for a job," the miserable, bound man said.

The young woman laughed.

"Not so, Pietro," she said. "But to be fair, the last time you saw me I was a skinny teenager with acne. I've grown up, you see."

His hand throbbed with pain, making it difficult for him to focus on what was happening. He tried to understand what she was saying.

"My name isn't Fiona Robinson, Pietro. My name is Jessica. Jessica Rossi."

Greco almost passed out from the pain in his hand and the shock of her words.

"Rossi?" he managed to stammer. "Jessica Rossi? You're his daughter?"

"Yes, Pietro. Jonathan Rossi, Don Rossi, to whom you swore allegiance, was my father. Don Rossi who you betrayed. The same man you murdered. And this," she said, picking up the severed digit, "is the finger that pulled the trigger."

Greco moaned in agony.

"You rode high for a long time, Pietro," she continued. "First in San Francisco as your Don's underboss and consigliere. Lately you've made a good start on building an empire in Alaska using money you stole from my father. Now the time has come for your journey to end. Now is the time for you to pay the price for betraying your Don."

As she spoke, she picked up a clamp. A tongue clamp.

An hour later, the Cessna 185 lifted off the water. The boat was left to drift with the tide.

It was quiet on board.

In Fairview, Jayne Colombo was again entering Dennis Caine's rundown apartment building. The building's exterior was raw and weathered with peeling paint. The landlord, whoever that might be, wasn't investing any money in upkeep.

Caine's apartment was as trashy inside as was the outside of the building. Jayne didn't really care. She didn't have to live there. She was only interested in the ability of these three people to effectively carry out her instructions.

She still hadn't decided what she would order them to do. That depended on Segal and what he did next. He hadn't confided in her in so many things. She was uncertain whether Trent Marshall was alive or dead. She wasn't sure who the people around Marshall's wife were. She only knew Segal wasn't being straight with her and she had to be prepared to protect herself.

She had called this evening's meeting to learn what her new team had in the way of weapons. Her own MAC 10 machine pistol was readily available in the oversized bag she always carried.

She again accepted Caine's offer of a beer, only to make her seem like part of the group.

She went straight to the point.

"So what do you guys have for guns?"

Dennis reached behind him and drew a small Beretta, which he laid on the table.

"Beretta 92 compact," he said, proudly. "Best features of a Beretta but smaller. Nine millimeter. Magazine holds ten rounds. Easy to hide. Plenty of kill power."

Jayne nodded. She wasn't an expert on guns but she knew Beretta made good weapons.

She looked at Brooke.

"What about you? You have a gun?"

Brooke reached for the long gun leaning against the wall near where she sat. She laid a lightweight weapon on the table.

".22 long rifle, .410 gauge, over and under," she said, describing the weapon. "It breaks down to fit in a bag like the one you're carrying."

Jayne was not impressed.

"Not much power in that," she said.

"If you're quiet and get close, it's deadly and doesn't make a lot of noise," Brooke replied, her cold eyes boring directly into Jayne's. "I'm quiet. I get close."

That was an explanation Jayne could understand.

J.B., the oldest of the three, laid a sawed-off double barrel shotgun on the table with the other weapons.

"At my age, I don't see well. I have to get close, too," he said, his small mouth stretched into that painful smile, "but I like to make a lot of noise. And this will do it. I find it has a chilling effect on the opposition."

She had questions about the weapons of choice exhibited by Brooke and J.B. but was convinced they wouldn't shy from pulling the trigger on whatever target she pointed them toward.

"OK, here's the first thing I want y'all to do," she said, laying a picture on the table. She had downloaded it from the Internet. It was a picture of Darcey Anderson taken from the website of her San Francisco design firm. "This woman is staying somewhere in town. I want to know where."

J.B. was quick to respond.

"That's a job for me. I'm good at that sort of thing. I'll find her for you and it won't take long."

August 3rd

The boat bobbed and drifted with the tides through the night and into the morning. Pushed back and forth through Icy Strait north of Chichagof Island.

Brian and Maureen Wayne were on the water at first light. They wanted to be back in Hoonah early. Maureen was on the city council. The council met as a Committee of the Whole on the first Thursday of the month. She wanted to be there by five o'clock.

They cruised slowly out of the protected harbor and into the waters of Icy Strait. Brian had the wheel. Maureen watched her hometown recede into the distance. Hoonah, originally known as Xunaa, which translates as "protection from the north wind," was largely populated by Tlingit people. Maureen's family had lived in the area since the 18th century. Part of Brian's family began trickling in a hundred years later.

They missed the drifting Sea Ray when they left that morning. They saw it as they were returning home at noon, their boat's locker filled with fish. It had been a good day.

Maureen had the wheel on the return. Brian was busy putting away their gear and straightening up. He would clean the deck and lockers more thoroughly when they were back in the harbor but he wanted to get a head start on the job before they got home.

"Brian, there's a boat over there," Maureen said. "Looks like a really fancy one."

Brian stopped what he was doing to look in the direction Maureen was pointing.

"What's he doing?" Brian wondered. "Looks like he's drifting."

"Maybe nobody's aboard," Maureen suggested. "It might have broken loose during the night. We should check to make sure."

"Yeah, that's a lot of boat to lose if there's nobody on board," her husband agreed.

Maureen pointed their bow toward the Sea Ray. When they were close enough, she skillfully guided it alongside.

"Hello!" Brian called out. "Anyone aboard?"

There was no answer.

"Get close enough for me to board her," he said.

Maureen moved in a little closer. Brian jumped onto the Sea Ray's deck and called out again.

"Anyone here?"

Still no answer.

"Check inside," Maureen suggested. "Someone might be hurt."

Brian disappeared into the cabin. She heard him make a sound. A gagging sound. Suddenly he rushed back onto the deck. He barely made it to the far side gunwale before vomiting into the sea.

Maureen was stunned.

"Brian, are you ok? What's in there?"

"You don't want to see it. Get the Coast Guard on the radio. Let them know we found a drifting boat with a body in the cabin. Better contact the State Troopers, too."

Jessica Rossi woke up late Thursday morning. After setting Greco adrift in his boat, they flew to Juneau, returned the rented Cessna, and caught an evening flight to San Francisco. Bell declared the shotgun in his checked luggage. TSA had no objection.

For the first time since she was a teenager she spent the night in her old bedroom. After her father was murdered, her mother saw to it that the family home in the hills of Atherton was well cared for. When Jessica said she planned to return to the California house, her mother asked a friend to stock the house with food and other items her daughter might need. There were still many who remained loyal to the Rossi family.

And, as Greco had learned, some of them pretended to be his friends as well. They were not.

Pulling a robe over her pajamas, Jessica went downstairs to the kitchen. She had programed the coffee pot before going to bed. Hot coffee would be waiting.

When her uncle came downstairs a short time later he found her sitting at her father's desk. She had already used her laptop to log on to the Internet.

"Everything good?" he asked, setting his own mug of coffee on the desk as he pulled a chair closer.

"Everything is very good," Jessica replied. "Our Miss Colombo has already logged on to her computer. The software I added is working perfectly."

"So what now?" he asked.

"Now we wait for Saturday night."

"And after that?" he continued.

"After that we finish off Greco's empire and get busy putting the Rossi family business back together."

"And you want me to be your consigliere or whatever it's called?" Bell said.

"No, I need your help, Uncle Jess," she said quickly, "but we're not going to use any of those old Mafia words. It's a new world and we will have a new family business. My only regret is that Pietro Greco won't know how much he is contributing to our business. As Shakespeare's Hamlet said, '... for tis the sport to have the enginer hoist with his own petard...'"

"And you, my dear niece, learned well the rest of Hamlet's speech," Bell added. "But I will delve one yard below their mines and blow them at the moon."

Jessica laughed at her uncle's completion of the quote.

"It's too bad my sister doesn't want to come back," Bell said. "This house and the grounds here are beautiful. And it was her home for so many years."

"That's why she isn't coming back. At least not right away. My father died here. In this room. It doesn't feel right to her."

Jessica stood and walked to the French doors leading to the garden and the pool.

"Daddy loved the garden," she remembered. "He enjoyed having lunch at the table out there. He said just being in the garden was soothing. Lash and I liked the pool better."

Bell chuckled at her reminiscence.

"Speaking of your brother, when will he join you here?"

Jessica's brother, Lash, was three years older. He was already in college when their father sent them with their mother to her family in Virginia.

He transferred to the University of Virginia to finish his undergraduate degree. He was now nearing completion of a master's degree in business at Tulane University's Freeman School of Business in New Orleans.

"He'll graduate at the end of the fall term," she said. "He will go to Virginia for a short visit and pick up a few belongings. He'll probably get here some time in February. And what he's learning at one of the country's best business schools will be very helpful."

"Just as your degree in computer science is already proving useful," Bell said, saluting her with his mug.

Jessica took a deep breath. It felt good to be home again.

The Coast Guard Cutter Liberty, on patrol near Chichagof Island, was the first to arrive. The cutter's commanding officer sent his lieutenant and two enlisted men to the Wayne's fishing boat. Brian and Maureen were both there. Brian refused to return to the Sea Ray.

"I didn't touch anything in the cabin," he said. "You couldn't make me touch anything in there. And I'm not going back on board that boat again. Nothing you can do will get me back on board that boat."

The lieutenant found that puzzling but didn't press the point. He gently pressed the nose of his small boat to the Sea Ray's stern. One of his crew leaped aboard the abandoned boat with a line, which he tied onto a cleat.

The lieutenant climbed onto the boat's deck and went into the cabin, followed by his crewman. In seconds, the enlisted man was back on deck, vomiting over the side just as Brian had done.

Inside, the lieutenant stood in a near state of shock at the sight. He wanted to run out of the cabin and vomit also. He was an officer. He didn't think he should do that. But he wanted to. Instead he stood frozen, struggling against the bile rising in his throat.

A man he had seen around Juneau was lying on a bench in the cabin. His arms spread-eagled, wrists tied to bolts screwed into the bulkhead.

He was missing the index finger on his right hand. His torso was covered in blood. His face was twisted into a picture of rage. It was as though he died screaming curses.

But he couldn't have died screaming curses. There was no way he could have done that.

On the small table near the bench lay the man's missing finger.

And something looking much like a human tongue.

Captain Van Patten called Monk as soon as he received the report from the commander of the Liberty.

"We found Greco's boat, Robert. And we found Greco. He's dead."

Robert was surprised.

"Any idea what happened? Could you tell how he died?"

"Oh yes, that wasn't hard to figure out," Van Patten replied with distaste. "He was died to a bulkhead. His index finger had been cut off."

"His trigger finger," Robert said. "That would be painful but wouldn't kill him."

"No, that's not what killed him. His tongue had been cut out, Robert. The only question is whether he bled out before he drowned in his own blood."

Robert felt a slight touch of nausea.

"Someone from his past executed him using his own boat as the gallows," he concluded.

"There's more, Robert," Van Patten continued. "He brought a young woman with him when he flew into town last week. She's nowhere to be found. Neither is Cameron McGraw, his restaurant manager here."

"They could be victims or perpetrators," Robert mused. "We don't have enough information to make that determination."

"We did learn one thing for certain," the Coast Guard captain said. "Acting on reason to enter, the Juneau police searched Greco's restaurant and the apartment above it. They found a hidden compartment in a closet. It contained only one item. A large item. A Remington Modular Sniper Rifle."

"So Greco was the one who shot Trent."

"I'd bet money on it. Since the bullet passed through Marshall's skull we don't have anything to compare. But it's about the right caliber and is good for the range. The sound and muzzle flash suppressors account for no one hearing or seeing the shot. And it's a very expensive weapon. It's doubtful that there's another like it in Juneau. Probably not anywhere in the state."

"Greco was afraid Trent would see him and recognize him so he tried to kill him. Really all he needed to do was stay out of sight for a short time. We were going to leave Juneau the next day. What a waste!" Robert lamented.

Caine's friend, J.B., called in the late afternoon. As promised, he had tracked Darcey Anderson to her "lair," as he called it.

"She's holed up in a luxurious penthouse condominium overlooking Bootlegger's Cove," he reported. "She has company. A man and woman are also staying there. And an older man comes and goes."

Colombo was surprised at how quickly J.B. had found the woman.

"I know people around town," was his only explanation.

"If she's in the penthouse, it'll be a secure floor," Colombo pointed out. "If, and I said if, I decide I want to get to her, how do we get onto that floor?"

"Oh, it might cost a few bucks in the right hands," J.B. answered. "Or a broken bone or two. I don't think that'll be a problem."

No one felt much like having dinner that evening. The image of Greco's finger and tongue lying on a table didn't encourage a healthy appetite.

Robert made pitcher of margaritas.

Then he made a second pitcher.

Darcey didn't go to the hospital. She was busy in the penthouse.

August 5th

Jessica Rossi had taken Greco's phone when they left him adrift in his boat.

It rang on Saturday night. Jessica's uncle answered.

"This is McGraw."

The woman who owned the Justice was calling.

"I need to talk to Segal," she said. "Put him on."

"He's...uh...busy. He can't come to the phone. And he told me to proceed with the transaction if you called to request it."

"Yeah, everything seems in order. You can transfer the funds."

McGraw ended the call and hit the speed dial for Jayne Colombo.

"Yeah," she answered, sounding unhappy. "Where are you?"

"This is McGraw, Jayne. You know where Jim is. And you know I'm not going to disturb him when he's having his fun."

She knew exactly what "fun" McGraw meant. The image of the young woman with the ridiculous red and black hair came to mind. It made the older woman furious.

"I just got the call from the Justice," he continued. "The skipper reports everything is in order. Jim told me to authorize you to transfer funds."

"I don't much like this," Colombo said. "If there's a problem it's going to be your head that rolls, not mine."

In her father's office in the Atherton house, Jessica watched everything Colombo was doing on her computer in the Anchorage office. Within seconds, the software the young woman had put on Colombo's machine captured everything Jessica needed to empty Greco's accounts. All the

160

passwords. The friendly banks who would follow instructions when they were given the correct passwords. Their coup was almost complete.

In a secluded cove on the coast of Admiralty Island, several boxes of pharmaceuticals were transferred from the larger supply vessel to be stowed in the compartments secreted below decks on the smaller yacht. The drugs were worth millions. All counterfeit. All promising death in the name of profit.

The next evening, Dancer would begin its journey north with a new crop of "wealthy travelers." On the following weekend, it was scheduled to meet another supplier to take on a cargo of electronics.

Smart phones. Tablets. Integrated circuit boards. Flash drives.

All counterfeit.

August 12th

It had been a long week.

The Coast Guard in Alaska and Seattle were anxious to move on Greco's small fleet. The FBI in Seattle were, too. Even the Alaska Bureau of Investigation and the police chiefs in Anchorage and Juneau were ready.

Monk still did his best to hold them back. He even convinced them to withhold any statements regarding Greco's death and the disappearance of Cameron McGraw and the unidentified young woman seen with Greco on his boat.

It wasn't time. He wasn't sure why. He just knew it wasn't time.

An old cop's instinct.

That changed at nine o'clock, Alaska Daylight Time.

Something happened.

Something big.

Half an hour earlier, Jessica Rossi was busy at her computer. Entering passwords. Accessing accounts in Greco's friendly banks. Moving funds to her own friendly banks. In less than 15 minutes she had set the charge that she earlier described in Shakespeare's words. She had "...delve[d] one yard below their mines to blow them at the moon."

Dancer and the ship from which it was to receive its cargo of counterfeit merchandise rode at anchor at yet another secluded cove. They were on the seaward side of Baranof Island, about halfway between Sitka and Port Alexander.

At the appointed hour, Captain Place dialed Greco's number. There was no answer.

The skipper of the larger vessel wasn't happy. This was a complication. People in his business didn't like complications.

Place nervously attempted to assuage his counterpart.

"These mobile phones can be a problem. My boss is probably not in range of a tower. I'll call the office."

Jayne Colombo was at her desk. She was not happy. She hadn't talked to her boss in over a week despite calling numerous times.

McGraw answered the first few times. Four days ago he called her to say that their boss was missing. He said he was calling the Coast Guard to report him overdue.

Since then she had heard nothing. When she called, no one answered. She could think of several possibilities. None of them good for her.

She became so alarmed that she considered calling the Coast Guard herself. But she was hesitant to get involved with anything resembling law enforcement.

When Place called to let her know their boss wasn't answering his phone, her glum mood took a turn toward the violent. She had to find out what was going on. But at this moment there was business to tend.

"I haven't been able to reach him either," she told Place. "But I'll make the transfer anyway. We can't stop because the boss found a new girlfriend."

Ending the call, she turned to her computer. She entered the necessary password to open the program that showed their accounts. That was the moment she realized how fundamentally her world had changed.

Each account showed a zero balance.

In a large, beautiful home south of San Francisco, the woman known as Fiona Robinson and her uncle, the man known as Cameron McGraw in Alaska, were sharing a bottle of Merlot from the well-stocked wine cellar. It had been a good night for them. Using connections with friendly banks supplied by her father's old friends and armed with all the passwords retrieved from Jayne Colombo's computer, Fiona had moved $21 million from Pietro Greco's banks into new accounts. Through a series of dummy corporations, the new accounts were all controlled by a previously unknown entity. The Bell Family Trust.

It had been a very good night.

In the secluded cove in Southeast Alaska, the two vessels bobbed side by side. On board Dancer, Captain Place was nervous. It had been an hour. The skipper of the boat with the cargo Place was to accept hadn't reappeared. Neither man had left the bridge of his vessel.

Place had no idea what was going on. Was it possible the transfer of funds hadn't been made? Even worse, had the transfer of funds been made and now the other captain planned to steal the cargo?

Place loved Dancer. He ran his hand over the beautiful, polished mahogany, caressed the brass fittings. He didn't want to see any harm come to her. He would fight to protect her.

Speaking softly, Place issued an order to his first officer. The man moved among the crew, repeating the captain's order.

Place himself reached into the locker beneath the wheel and reached for the AR-15, keeping the rifle out of sight as he leaned it against the bulkhead within easy reach. His crew did the same. Place knew his orders were to avoid a fight but he might not have the choice.

If they had to fight, he would regret only that Greco hadn't supplied them with automatic weapons. He feared they were outgunned.

In the office of the Anchorage restaurant, Jayne Colombo sat for several minutes in stunned silence. She stared at the screen of her computer as though willing the lines of zeros to turn themselves back into the millions they had been.

At last a horrible shriek came from deep inside her. She swept her arms across the desk, scattering everything on it. She stood and stomped around the room, throwing anything she could reach.

She shouted curses. She excoriated everyone who came to mind, starting with Pietro Greco. And yes, she reverted to calling him by his name. What a fool he was. He let someone take a fortune from him. Either that or he stole it himself, leaving her to take the fall for who knows what.

She cursed Cameron McGraw and Fiona Robinson, the only names she knew for them.

She cursed Trent Marshall, whose appearance in Juneau had been the catalyst for the crash of Greco's empire.

Marshall! She didn't know if he was dead or alive. But his wife was alive. And Colombo knew where to find her.

There were things to do before she could think about Marshall's wife.

She opened the small safe tucked into a corner of the office. She knew Greco kept some cash on hand. There was almost fifty thousand dollars. She stuffed the cash into the oversized bag she carried.

The restaurant's checkbook was also in the safe. There was another fifty thousand in that account and she was a signer on the checks. She put the checkbook in her bag as well.

She called Caine and told him not to bother coming to work the next day. The restaurant was closing. She gave him no more details except to say she would have a job for him soon. She didn't tell him she had no intention of paying him for the job nor did she let him know she would kill him when the job was done. She made a crude sign saying "Due to Unforeseen Circumstances JS Bistro Is Temporarily Closed. Will Reopen Soon."

She found a stool at the bar where she sat in the dark drinking scotch.

Captain Place told one of his crew to check the anchor line.

"Feels like we might be drifting a little," he lied.

The crewman didn't like the order but feared his captain's discipline more if he disobeyed. He stepped out on deck.

On the larger vessel, the skipper watched as the crewman stepped into the open. He brought his Smith & Wesson Model 25-5 .45 caliber long barrel revolver to bear and fired. The crewman was knocked off his feet. He tumbled into the sea.

With the captain's shot, his crew opened up on the yacht. Smashing glass, splintering wood with a hail of bullets. The long barrel revolvers were effective weapons given the range of fire. The extra length added punch to the .45 caliber rounds.

Captain Place was appalled as he watched his precious Dancer being rapidly shot to pieces. He ordered his men to return fire.

Dancer's crew was more heavily armed with their AR–15s. Unfortunately for them, they came to the fight with too little experience.

The three so-called male guests rushed to join the fight, armed with the rifles they were given when they came aboard. In one of the cabins, the three women guests, all of whom were hookers from Seattle, lay on the floor, holding each other, as they listened to the battle raging around them.

The skipper of the larger vessel ordered two of his men who he knew to be better than average marksmen to aim at Dancer's waterline. He would sink the yacht to repay them for reneging on their agreement.

Captain Place saw the two crewmen using two of the ship's hatches to steady their long barrel revolvers. He saw their angle of fire. He realized they had been ordered to sink Dancer.

"No," he shouted, as he ran from the bridge onto his own deck. "No, you won't sink my ship!"

He fired as he ran. It was the first time he had ever experienced a gunfight. He lost control of himself. His shots went wide, doing no damage to vessel or personnel.

This was not his counterpart's first fight. He realized he had the opposing commander in position to be taken out. He stepped onto the deck and aimed.

His first bullet struck Place in his right foot, slowing his charge across the deck. The wounded man was hit a second time in his left elbow, shattering the union of the humerus, radius, and ulna. His left arm now useless, Place stood bleeding and helpless, unable to raise his rifle into firing position.

The captain on the opposing vessel, smiled and gave Place a mock salute. Then he shot Dancer's skipper squarely in the chest. He calmly turned and stepped back into the bridge of his own vessel.

The cove in which the fight was taking place was only a few miles from the small community of Port Alexander. Guests at a luxury fishing lodge were enjoying a night cap in the bar when they heard the sound of gunfire. The guests, most taking their drinks with them, followed the lodge staff when they stepped outside to better hear the racket.

"Sounds like a full-scale war," one of the guests said.

"Sure does," the lodge owner said. "I'm calling the Troopers."

The Coast Guard had three Sikorsky Jayhawk helicopters. At the request of the State Troopers, Captain Van Patten ordered two of them to fly the seaward coast of Baranof Island and find the altercation. He ordered the third to standby in reserve.

It was roughly sixty miles from Sitka to Port Alexander. The Jayhawks would cruise at 140 knots, or 161 miles per hour. They would cover the island's coast in well under an hour.

He also ordered the Cutter Bailey Barco and a buoy tender from Ketchikan to Baranof Island. They would be guided by the crews of the choppers once they located the source of the gunfire. The Bailey Barco, which could cruise at twenty-eight knots, or about thirty-two miles an hour, would arrive four and a half hours later. The slower buoy tender sometime after that.

The choppers and the Cutter were both armed with medium machine guns. They were prepared to do battle or rescue survivors. Or both.

The Jayhawks flew with starboard doors open, machine guns at the ready. Each member of the crew was armed with an M4 fully automatic rifle and a Sig Sauer P226 semiautomatic handgun.

Three State Troopers were in the lead chopper, adding their arms to the mix. Each Trooper carried a Glock. One held a Remington 870 shotgun, the second an AR–15 rifle, the third a Heckler & Koch MP5 submachine gun. All standard issue for the troopers.

Unlike Captain Place and his crew, the Troopers knew how to use the AR–15 and their other weapons.

Half an hour into the flight, those aboard the helicopters heard the faint sound of gunfire, muffled by the sound of the rotors and the rush of air going by the open doors.

The pilots turned toward the sound of the guns as best they could figure it. It was the light from a burning vessel that pinpointed their destination.

The pilot of the lead aircraft held them at the cove's entrance while he surveyed the dramatic scene below. A yacht, flames shooting from the main cabin, was listing heavily to starboard. A larger vessel lay alongside, its crew continuing to fire rounds from long barreled revolvers into the already defeated smaller boat.

The pilot issued orders to the second aircraft, then pushed his chopper toward the fight. Using the bullhorn feature of his communications system, he directed that fighting cease and ordered the combatants to lay down their weapons.

When a foolish crewman on the apparently victorious vessel raised his weapon toward the helicopter, the pilot didn't hesitate to give the order to fire as he swung his aircraft to port. The two men manning the M240 machine gun in the open starboard door sent a stream of bullets into the fight. They raked the deck with the machine gun, watching four of the exposed crew drop. Realizing they were heavily outclassed, the remainder began dropping their weapons to the deck and raising their hands.

The skipper, furious at being denied his victory and unwilling to be taken captive by the Americans, stood in the entrance to his ship's bridge, firing ineffectively at the helicopter. State Trooper Corporal Susan Duryea braced herself against the aircraft's door, taking careful aim with her AR-15. Duryea was an expert with the rifle. Taking windage and elevation into account as well as the up and down movement of her target's ship, she fired three rounds in quick succession. All three struck the belligerent seaman in the chest. A pattern of hits close enough for Duryea's hand to cover.

Duryea had an interest in the events that had unfolded in recent days. She was suspicious of Jim Segal the day the two men were shot at Auke Bay but had let herself be convinced he wasn't a problem. She let him go then. If only she had pressed him that day so much of what had happened might have been prevented. What was turning out to be a major smuggling operation could have been shut down much sooner.

The lead pilot lowered his aircraft, allowing the State Troopers to leap onto the deck. They began rounding up the crew, checking the wounded to determine who was still alive and who was not.

Meanwhile, the second helicopter focused on the yacht, which was clearly on the verge of sinking. Three women, one middle aged, slightly overweight man dressed as a passenger, and two younger men, probably crew, were clinging to the deeply slanted deck.

If they couldn't be rescued before Dancer sank, they would go into a state of shock within the first minute of immersion in the cold water, leading to the possibility of heart failure. If their hearts weren't overpowered by the immediate shock, they could survive as long as thirty minutes. But that was risky. After ten minutes their body temperatures would be lowered to the extent that the effort required to swim or tread water would become more and more difficult.

While the pilot hovered above the sinking boat, the crew dismounted the machine gun and stowed it. They broke out the rescue basket and hooked it up to be lowered. They tapped the pilot on the shoulder to let him know the basket was ready.

The pilot activated the loudspeaker function of his communications system again, directing the six people clinging to the boat to get into the basket one at a time, starting with the women.

The basket was lowered, the first woman climbed in and was pulled up to the helicopter. Over the next half hour, all six were lifted from the doomed vessel. Twenty minutes later, Dancer slipped beneath the waves on her way to the bottom. Captain Place remained aboard as she sank.

The chopper with the survivors from Dancer started back for Sitka. They would arrange for medical care and, as the six were suspected of being part of a smuggling operation, for incarceration pending investigation.

The crew would refuel and return to the cove to assist their companion aircraft. The two aircraft would take turns maintaining watch over the surviving vessel until the arrival of the Bailey Barco.

The State Troopers aboard the ship had opened some of the boxes stacked on deck. They were filled with electronic equipment. Video games. Tablets. Integrated circuit boards. Flash drives. All brand names. All either stolen or counterfeit. Most likely counterfeit.

The Troopers were the first to witness firsthand Greco's smuggling operation. The conspiracy he had launched while posing as Jim Segal, successful businessman and restaurateur.

Though it was late, Van Patten called Monk to report on the evening's activities.

"Now it's time," Monk said.

"Time for what?" Van Patten asked. He knew Monk had been doing everything he could to keep the Coast Guard, FBI, State Troopers, and local police from taking action over the past week. He didn't know why Monk wanted them to hold back but he trusted the old cop's judgment.

"Something has happened," Monk said. "Greco's operation has been brought into the open. His remaining people will be confused and scared. We need to increase their confusion. Scare them more."

"What do you suggest we do, Robert?"

"Tomorrow morning is the time for the Troopers to announce the grisly murder of Jim Segal, reveal his true identity, and report the disappearance of Cameron McGraw and Fiona Robinson."

"Yeah, now it's time," he said aloud as he ended the call.

August 13th

It was unusual for a press conference to be called on a Sunday.

Commissioner of Public Safety Val Murphy caught the early flight to Anchorage. Captain Van Patten traveled with him. They arrived shortly after nine o'clock Sunday morning.

In Anchorage they were joined by APD Chief Ben Kline, Tom Wofford, FBI Special Agent in Charge for Alaska, and Captain Doc Williams of the State Troopers Bureau of Investigation. Williams was once a highly decorated Navy corpsman attached to a Marine unit. He was still called Doc as a mark of respect.

At two o'clock Sunday afternoon, the room was filled with representatives of Alaska's print and broadcast media. Others from around the state joined the session via teleconference. Commissioner Murphy opened the conference by announcing the death of the man known in Alaska as Jim Segal. He then turned it over to SAiC Wofford.

"Jim Segal's real name was Pietro Greco," Wofford said.

As Wofford revealed all they knew about Pietro Greco, a buzz went through the gathering of reporters. Several of them had dined at JS Bistro and knew him as Jim Segal.

The room became quiet, though no less attentive, when Van Patten described the gruesome scene the Coast Guard found when they boarded Greco's boat. He also noted the disappearance of Cameron McGraw and Fiona Robinson. With regret, he said they did know if the two were victims or perpetrators.

The captain then announced the discovery of Greco's smuggling operation. Doc Williams described the fight on the coast of Baranof Island resulting in the sinking of the yacht Dancer. He limned the cargo

170

of counterfeit goods the State Troopers found when they boarded the surviving ship.

When Williams concluded his remarks, the room was silent for several seconds. Then it erupted into chaos as the officials were deluged with questions.

Finally, Commissioner Murphy brought the conference to a close by announcing that the combined law enforcement agencies of the states of Alaska and Washington, the FBI, and the Coast Guard were immediately launching a joint effort to shut down the remainder of Greco's criminal activities and take into custody everyone involved. Even at that moment, Murphy said, the effort was underway in the San Juan Islands.

It was a cloudy, cool day in Anchorage. Robert made the decision that the cocktail of the day would be bourbon on the rocks. It was a day of forceful action. He thought it should it be paired with a cocktail equal in force.

He poured the drinks while the group in the Anchorage penthouse, at Robert's insistence, gathered around the large screen television in the main sitting room to watch the evening news.

At the end of the report, the group of friends clinked their glasses together. Pietro Greco had paid for shooting Trent. His empire was being disassembled.

He had also paid for other sins. They could only guess what those sins might have been.

Jayne Colombo watched the news in her Spenard apartment. Once again, she couldn't believe what she was seeing and hearing. How could this have happened? How could Greco be so stupid as to let himself get murdered?

The thought set her off again perseverating Pietro Greco. It had become a daily ritual.

She knew it did no good. Greco was gone. He wasn't coming back. His smuggling operation was broken.

One of the yachts was lying on the bottom of the sea in a Southeast Alaska fjord. The others were likely tied up at the abandoned dock in the San Juans, oblivious that they were out of work.

She could change that and maybe salvage something out of the mess Greco had made. She picked up her phone and dialed a number with a 206 area code.

The workers in the old warehouse on the abandoned dock in the San Juan Islands looked up into the dusk of the evening sky as they heard the sound of the helicopters. Two Coast Guard Dolphins had been dispatched from their base at Port Angeles. On arriving at Greco's confiscated island they found his workers moving as fast as they could to load cargo onto the three remaining yachts and a beat-up commercial fishing boat used to ferry counterfeit merchandise to the Port of Seattle.

As the choppers drew closer to the island, the yachts and the fishing boat attempted to start their engines and put to sea. While one of the Dolphins hovered to provide covering fire if needed, the second swung to bring the Herstal M240 belt fed machine gun mounted in the starboard doorway to bear on the fleeing vessels.

Firing at a rate of six hundred rounds per minute, the machine gun chewed up the water, sending hundreds of mini tsunamis splashing onto the decks.

If anyone on the four boats thought they could outrun the rounds being thrown at them, the skippers quickly learned otherwise. Three Coast Guard cutters, armed with heavier machine guns and grenade launchers, came into view. Two circled in from the west side of the island, the third from the east. Escape was completely cut off.

All four skippers killed their engines, letting their vessels settle heavily back into the water. All four stepped onto open decks with arms raised, surrendering their boats. The AR-15s with which all four were armed remained locked away.

When the helicopters settled onto firm ground, FBI agents and armed Coast Guardsmen swarmed around and into the old building. The workers were arrested and handcuffed.

The yachts and fishing boat, now completely docile, returned to the dock. The captains and crews were taken into custody.

As the warehouse and boats were searched, ladies' fashions, jewelry, and shoes, all designer brands and all counterfeit, were found. With more relief, the FBI agents searching the warehouse discovered counterfeit drugs worth millions. Fake products that would have killed the most vulnerable.

All telephones were seized. An observant agent noticed one had received a call from an Anchorage number within the past two hours. The agent turned the phone over to his boss, who dialed the number.

Jayne Colombo was surprised when her phone rang. The call was from the number she had called to warn the people on the island to pack up and get out. She hesitated to answer. It could be good news. Probably not.

She let it go to voice mail.

The phone was a burner. Whoever was calling would hear only a standard greeting. They would not hear her voice. They wouldn't know who they were calling. They couldn't trace it to her.

The message left on her phone was another notice of disaster.

"This is Charles Cabot, FBI Special Agent in Charge for the Seattle District. Whoever receives this message should know that we have taken control of an old warehouse full of counterfeit products on a deserted island in the San Juans. We have also seized three yachts and a fishing boat. More than one of those we have taken into custody are anxious to tell us anything we want to know. You are out of business and will soon be in custody. Have a nice day."

Colombo threw the phone across the room. For two long minutes she stood in the middle of the room, trembling. Unable to move. Trying to think.

She was running out of options. Boxed in. Escape was being cut off in every direction. Her chances were slim.

She had planned to go to the bank as soon as it opened the following day to withdraw most of the funds from the restaurant's account, leaving only enough to keep the account going. Now that was out of the question. People at the bank would have seen the same news report she saw. Any attempt now to withdraw such a large sum from that account would only send the cops to her door faster. She had only the money she found in the safe.

She poured another scotch.

There was nothing left for her but to seek revenge.

Greco dead. McGraw and that little twit Fiona nowhere to be found. Marshall either dead or on life support. Only Marshall's wife was left as target of Colombo's fury.

She drained her glass and poured another drink. She had to stop her hand from shaking before doing what she intended next.

When she felt in control, she called Caine. She told him they had a job to do the following night. She told him to pick up breakfast and bring it, along with Brooke and J.B., to her apartment by eight o'clock the next morning. Then she told him to put J.B. on the line.

Two hours later, J.B. pressed the buzzer asking for entry into the lobby of the building overlooking Cook Inlet. He had made it a point to meet and become friendly with the night concierge, dropping in over the past few evenings with coffee and doughnuts.

At the sound of the buzzer, the man looked up from the book he was reading. He was over sixty, bespectacled, and wore his silver hair long, matching it with a silver beard. He was among the thousands who reached retirement age only to discover they didn't have the financial resources they thought they would have. Consequently, he was working well past his prime to keep food in his belly.

J.B. was about the same age as the concierge. He had an intimate understanding of the man's life situation. His thin gray hair was a hint that he shared the fate of the concierge. It was why he had to sleep on the couch in the small apartment he shared with two roommates. Fortunately, he was as murderous as were they.

J.B. smiled his humorless, painful smile as the man opened the door.

"Good evening, Trey. How's your world this evening?"

"Doing ok, J.B.," the old man replied. "No doughnuts tonight?"

"Oh, I have something much better than doughnuts."

When he left half an hour later, J.B. had what he came for in his pocket. Trey had been offered a choice. Two thousand of Colombo's scarce dollars or considerable pain. The old man opted for the money, understanding he would also get the pain from J.B.'s partners if he told anyone about their transaction.

J.B.'s partners were not known to him. The money was tactile in Trey's hands. He understood that pain could have a certain tactile nature of its own. It was a thought that, at his age, he couldn't face.

August 14th

Monday morning broke cloudy but comfortable in Anchorage. Caine and his companions arrived at Colombo's Spenard apartment at a quarter past eight.

She had not slept all night. She was on edge and furious that they were fifteen minutes late. With great effort she held her fury inside. She needed them to storm Darcey Anderson's penthouse that night.

They would pay later. J.B. would die immediately. The other two after she had her fun with them. She was looking forward to the fun. It excited her to think of it. But now was not the time for fantasizing.

They ate biscuits stuffed with bacon, eggs, and cheese along with fried frozen hash browns as she briefed them on her plan. Over the next two hours they burned through three pots of coffee as she made them go over the plan time and again. All three had to know their parts without having to think.

Each member of Colombo's hastily assembled team reacted differently.

J.B. seemed resigned. He realized his neck was already in a noose as Trey could, and no doubt would if pressured, identify him as the front man. Trey would have to die.

Brooke seemed excited. Her nostrils flared. Her breathing grew faster. Colombo decided Brooke was as perverted as was she. It made her think again of the fun they might have before the younger woman died.

Surprisingly, Caine seemed the most troubled. Negative. Almost frightened.

"Are you sure this is a good idea, Jayne?" he questioned.

"What's wrong? Scared?"

"No, I'm not scared," he said, offended. "It just seems like a wild plan to me. And for what purpose?"

175

"For my purpose, Dennis," Colombo said. "That's all that should concern you."

She saw Caine fading from her fantasy. Maybe the fun would include only Brooke. Caine didn't seem as interesting as she once thought.

The cloudy day covered the magnificent view from the penthouse. Robert, Christopher, and Nancy were gathered again in the main sitting room for coffee. Darcey was busy making her morning phone call to Louisiana. And with other things.

Captain Nettleton from the Seattle PD had called Christopher to tell him that, with information supplied by some of those arrested the evening before, they had carried out a raid on a rundown warehouse on the waterfront.

They had seized another old commercial fishing boat and a retired tug. Greco had used those nondescript vessels to lighter his counterfeit goods in from the island. From there they were picked up by independent dealers in vans and small trucks that could move unnoticed along the waterfront.

"Our holding cells are full of former Greco employees," Nettleton said, with satisfaction. "And almost all of them can't wait to tell their stories. They're especially anxious since they learned the district attorney is exploring charges of something like serial attempted murder or whatever he can find similar to it."

"Intent to distribute that much in counterfeit drugs has to be considered at least assault with a deadly weapon," Christopher suggested.

He had put his phone on speaker so the others could listen to the conversation.

"If any of them are ill, or become ill, you could always treat them with their own drugs," Robert chimed in.

"Well, that would be justice. But vigilante justice," Nettleton said. "The DA wouldn't go for it."

"No more than they deserve," the old cop responded.

"Can't say I disagree, Colonel Monk," Nettleton said. "But I guess we have to play it by the book. We'll nail 'em all on something."

After the call from Nettleton the atmosphere in the room was considerably lighter than it had been in weeks.

"What are we doing for dinner?" Christopher asked. "We should do something special."

"We are doing something special," Nancy said. "Darcey has been teaching me to make real southern fried chicken. And I'm making it tonight with mashed potatoes and gravy and lima beans on the side. Is that special enough for you?"

"Oh yeah, a California girl learning to cook southern!" Christopher said, a genuinely happy grin spreading across his wide face. "That's very special!"

Christopher thought the days of pizza and scrambled eggs and ham sandwiches at their house were over.

"We'll do even better than that," Darcey said, overhearing the last of the conversation as she entered the room. "I'll make French 75s and we'll toast Trent."

'Fried chicken and French 75s," Robert said, with delight. "I'm in. I'm definitely in."

Colombo and her team walked up to the building overlooking Cook Inlet at precisely nine o'clock. She chose that hour thinking Darcey Anderson Marshall and her guests would have had a few cocktails and, if luck was with the attackers, a heavy dinner. Hopefully they would be sluggish and slow to respond.

Trey had given J.B. the pass keys that would let them enter the main floor lobby, use the elevator to access the secured floors at the top of the building, and enter all the condominiums in the building. He also gave him the floor plan of the four thousand square foot penthouse Darcey was occupying along with its adjoining one thousand square foot caretaker's apartment.

Colombo knew there were two entrances. One was through the main front door, the second from the caretaker's apartment through a small, informal sitting room to the rear of the penthouse.

The concierge looked up at the sound of the door opening. He saw J.B. entering accompanied by another man with uncombed brown hair and rumpled clothing, a brassy blonde woman with a crazy look about her, and a smaller, younger woman with dark hair and cold eyes.

J.B was old fashioned. He always appeared in public neatly and conservatively dressed in a coat and tie. Tonight was no different except for the duffle bag he carried.

Both women carried oversized handbags. The younger woman wore jeans and a light, pullover sweater. The older woman wore a dark skirt cut high above her knees and a white top under her fashionable jacket. Both were dressed for easy maneuverability.

"Good evening, Trey," J.B. said, the ever present, painful smile on his thin face. "I've brought some friends to meet you tonight. This young lady is Brooke. She came along especially to thank you for helping us."

"That...that's nice of you, J.B. but it isn't necessary," Trey stammered. This didn't feel right. This felt dangerous. He was suddenly fearful.

"Nonsense," J.B. said. "We always take good care of our friends. You just take Brooke into that back office for a while. I guarantee it'll be an experience you'll remember for the rest of your life."

Brooke didn't wait for the old man to take the lead. Without speaking a word, she reached out and took his hand, leading him to the vacant office behind the concierge desk. Trey noticed that the cold look in her eyes got no warmer.

The door was closed no longer than a few seconds when those waiting in the lobby heard a faint pop. Brooke reappeared, the oversized bag hanging from her shoulder, the lightweight, long gun broken as she replaced the .22 long rifle cartridge she had just used to send a bullet through the ear and directly into the center of Trey's brain.

J.B. was right. It was an experience Trey remembered for the few seconds that remained of his life.

Upstairs in the penthouse, Robert was preparing to take the trash to the garbage chute around the corner from the elevator.

Nancy was in the kitchen finishing the cleanup from dinner. Christopher was helping but had taken a short break to go to their room.

She was pleased with the dinner she'd made. The fried chicken, flour seasoned with cayenne and buttermilk with a little maple syrup as the liquid was a big hit. She also had the idea to sauté a chopped green onion until it was soft and mix it in with the mashed potatoes. That proved to be popular also.

The oil in which the chicken was cooked was still far too hot to handle without risking a serious burn. They would leave that to cool overnight and clean the pan in the morning.

Darcey was busy elsewhere in the penthouse.

Colombo and her four accomplices rode the elevator to the top floor. There they took up their assigned positions.

Caine, backed by J.B., was assigned to go in through the front door. Colombo and Brooke would take the stealth approach through the caretaker's apartment. They would have Darcey Anderson Marshall and her companions in a crossfire.

Caine and J.B. took up their positions. They watched as the two women entered the caretaker's apartment. They gave them three minutes, as directed, to locate the rear entrance into the penthouse.

Caine used the time to work the slide of his Beretta. J.B. unzipped the duffle bag and brought out his shotgun, breaking it to assure himself each chamber was ready with a twelve gauge shell.

When exactly three minutes had passed, Caine used his pass key to open the front door of the penthouse. He quietly pushed the door open and stepped into the large entry way.

He found himself face to face with Robert Monk.

Robert had been in many violent situations in his long career. He was surprised but less so than Caine. That gave the old cop time to drop to the ground, reaching to his lower leg to free the Glock from its hideout holster.

In the few seconds it took Robert to arm and cock his own weapon, Caine fired. The man lying on the floor was hit in the side, blood immediately beginning to flow.

Caine fired only once. Again the experience of the retired cop prevailed. Robert fired three times. The first round hit Caine in the left ankle, taking his leg out from under him. The second struck his left wrist as he fell backward. Before he could raise the Beretta to fire again, Robert's third shot hit him square in the lower belly.

Caine was out of the fight. The bullet to his belly bored through his small intestine. He didn't know it yet but he was dead. It would be a slow, painful death.

When Caine fell, he crashed into J.B., who was following too closely behind him. One barrel of the older man's shotgun fired into the ceiling.

Before he could right himself and train the second loaded barrel at Robert, Nancy came from the kitchen to the left of the doorway.

Unfortunately for J.B. her opening shot was a large frying pan full of hot cooking oil tossed directly at him.

J.B. screamed as the hot oil covered his head, face and body. In his agony he waved the shotgun around wildly, blindly seeking a target to avenge his agony. His inability to find a target gave Nancy the opportunity to draw her Smith & Wesson .357 magnum. She sent one bullet from the revolver into J.B.'s left hip, shattering the femur at its juncture with the pelvic structure. A permanently crippling wound.

All thought of continuing the fight was gone. J.B. was scalded, blinded, unable to stand, and now unable to even find the shotgun which he had dropped when Nancy's bullet broke his hip. He lay moaning and crying on the floor, covered by hot oil turning his flesh into something resembling hamburger, blood pouring from his wounded leg.

Brooke had told Colombo that being quiet and getting close with her lightweight weapon was her specialty. And so it was.

She had entered through the caretaker's apartment and was now standing only a few feet behind Nancy, the top barrel of her light, two barreled weapon, with its .22 caliber long rifle cartridge, was cocked. Focused on the two at the front door, the former detective sergeant was unaware of the other woman's presence.

At that moment, Detective Captain Christopher Booth stepped into the hallway. Drawing his own Glock, he entered the fray in time to save his partner. Booth fired twice. His first bullet penetrated the flesh high on Brooke's left shoulder to the right of her shoulder blade. Excruciating but not a killing shot. Her lips turned up in a smile. The pain didn't appear to bother her. It seemed to thrill her.

Brooke turned to train her weapon on a new target but she was out of time. Booth fired again. His second shot penetrated her heart. The woman's eyes began to glaze over as she dropped to her knees. She fired her light weapon but the small piece of lead buried itself harmlessly in the ceiling. Her fingers twitched as she tried to switch barrels to fire the second round. But they stopped moving as the light went out of her eyes.

The obstreperous activity brought Darcey from the master bedroom, the single shot .410 gauge hand gun at the ready. She was in time to confront Jayne Colombo.

Colombo was delighted. Darcey was her main target. Trent Marshall's wife was to be Colombo's revenge. She held her MAC 10 at the ready. But Darcey fired first.

Her shot was accurate. The small shot from Darcey's unusual weapon spread a series of red dots across Colombo's chest. But it wasn't a killing blow. The .410 gauge was little more than birdshot. It stung but did no serious danger.

Colombo looked down and laughed.

"That's not much of a gun, Mrs. Marshall," she taunted. "I think I have you."

Colombo waved her machine pistol at Darcey. She wanted to make this moment last. She was shocked when she heard the voice behind her.

"Let her go," the voice said. "It's me you want. Not her."

In her surprise, Colombo spun to face the voice. The voice came from the dimly lit shadow of a doorway.

She could see only the outline of a man. He was seated. He seemed to be wearing a hat. A dark western style hat with a pinched front crown, brim turned slightly down in front, with gentle upward curls on the sides.

"Marshall? Is that you? You're alive?" Colombo questioned, hardly believing it.

"I'm alive."

Colombo felt perverted desire stirring within. Her breath became ragged.

"This is perfect," she said, her voice husky. "We can have a little fun as we die. All three of us."

"It's me you want," the voice repeated. "But not that way."

"No fun? How disappointing," she said. "Just death then. First her. Then you."

She pointed the notoriously inaccurate MAC 10 machine pistol toward Darcey. She saw the flame from the barrel of the revolver held by the shadowy figure at the end of the hallway. She heard the sound of metal exploding powder. She watched in disbelief as the man disappeared in a cloud of black smoke. All that before she felt the .44 caliber ball strike her lower left leg, breaking the tibia.

She pulled the trigger of her MAC 10 as she fell to the ground. Though hurting badly, she had time to do so. The weapon the man was using was not a modern handgun. It fired slowly. The three round burst from her weapon went wide to the side of the dim figure sitting in the cloud of dark smoke.

She saw the burst of flame from the center of the cloud as Marshall fired again. The second ball hit Colombo in the upper left arm, plowing through muscle and nicking the humerus. She was no longer able to use that arm to steady her weapon.

"Toss it away," the voice masked in darkness and burned black powder ordered. "Your fight is over."

Colombo had no remaining ability to reason. She attempted to raise the MAC 10 again, using only her right arm.

A third time the handgun fired. The third ball struck Colombo in the neck, perforating the right carotid artery, crushing the junction where the main artery split into the external and internal vessels. Blood that should be going to her brain was gushing onto the floor as the woman collapsed. She would bleed out within minutes.

Robert watched Colombo fall from where he lay near the front door. Christopher was tending his wound, pressing a handkerchief against it to stop the bleeding. Having ascertained that Caine was dead, Nancy was attempting to help J.B. There was little she could do to ease his agony.

APD Chief Ben Kline rode in the ambulance transporting Monk to the closest hospital.

"Looks like the bullet went straight through, Robert. Didn't hit anything important. Good thing you have so much fat around your belly," Kline joked. "Probably saved your life."

"It's all the time I've spent with Darcey this summer. These folks eat well. I could get fatter if I spent more time with them."

Three of the attackers were dead. J.B. would live out what remained of his life blinded, disfigured, and wheel chair bound in an Alaska state prison hospital.

"This wraps it up, Robert," Kline said. "The last of Greco's operation. Jayne Colombo was his right hand here in Anchorage. There's no one left."

"That woman Colombo said some strange things before she died," Robert said. "If you run her DNA you might find a similarity to your serial killer. Just an old cop's instinct."

"Now that would be a bonus," Kline said, "and it really would wrap things up."

"There's still the matter of the attack on Darcey's family in Louisiana," Monk reminded him.

"Just some local thugs from what I hear," Kline said. "I think the sheriff and the New Orleans cop who was involved can handle them."

"We'll see," Robert said.

When the police and EMS personnel were gone, Trent Marshall lifted himself slowly from the wheel chair and walked unsteadily but with determination to the couch in the main sitting area. Darcey joined him. For the first time in weeks, he put his arm around her.

"This was a beautiful place, Darcey," he said.

"I thought you'd like it," she responded. "It was better without the bullet holes and blood. Not to mention the stink and stain of black powder from that silly revolver you fired."

"It's not silly," he protested. "It's a reproduction of a LeMat revolver, a very fine 19th century weapon."

"It's black powder, Trent. It stinks and stains."

He looked back toward the doorway from which he had fired the revolver. Black smoke lingered there despite the door leading to the deck and the windows that Darcey had opened.

"Well, yeah, I guess it does," he admitted. "We'll have to pay for the damages. It might be cheaper to buy this place."

"I already did."

"You what?" he asked, incredulously.

"I already bought it," she said calmly. "I knew you were going to live and I thought it would be nice to have a place where we could have a white Christmas."

"And if I didn't make it?"

"I never let myself consider that possibility," she said. "But if that was to be the way of it, then it would have been nice to have a place here in Anchorage. The place where you left us, if that was what happened. A place I could come alone and remember our life together."

"But without even talking to me? You bought it?"

"I told you about it," she explained. "You didn't say no."

"Darcey, I was in a coma."

"Dr. Shannon said it was possible you could hear things. I figured you would hear me and if you didn't like the idea you would find a way to let me know. And you didn't," she continued. "So you didn't say no."

"The other residents of the building might not be happy with us moving in," Trent pointed out. "Is there an association that has to approve us?"

"That could be a problem," Darcey admitted.

Trent looked at his wife. He looked around at what might be their new penthouse. He looked back at Darcey.

"How many homes do you think we need, Darcey?" he asked.

"I'd say three ought to do it."

Trent looked around again. He considered the magnificent view. He remembered how it looked without the bullet holes and blood on the floor.

"Well, how about a white Christmas then," he said, flashing the old wide smile Darcey knew so well.

"I'll call Miles first thing tomorrow and tell him he has to come to Alaska. He has work to do."

Miles Diaz-Douglas, chief operating officer of Darcey's design firm with offices in San Francisco and New Orleans, had been outraged that he wasn't allowed to come north with the others. Darcey knew he would be thrilled at the prospect of stripping the new penthouse down to the studs in the wall and rebuilding it from scratch.

She also knew he would be clamoring to open an Anchorage office. She thought about the view of the Sleeping Lady, the Alaska Range, and Denali from their deck. An Anchorage branch of DJA Designs could work.

"I think you should leave the hat here," she said, looking him over. "I think white snow melting and dripping off a black Stetson would be sexy."

"Yeah, I like the image," Trent said.

August 22nd

It was another hot day in the old town when Sheriff Jack Blake walked into the small hospital. Dr. Donald Brand met him in the lobby.

"Where is he, Donald?" the sheriff asked.

"Third room on the right, Jack," the doctor said.

"Can he talk?"

"He can talk," the doctor said, "but take it easy with him. It was as bad as it gets as heart attacks go. He won't last long."

"It won't be a great loss, Donald."

"I suppose you're right, Jack," the doctor replied, sadly. "But we have different jobs. I hate to lose a patient. Even a bad one."

"That old man in there dying and his bone breaking sons sent you a lot of patients over the years, Donald. This parish will be all the better with them gone."

Brand didn't disagree.

Sheriff Blake stood in the door of old man Garth's room. He didn't like to be in the same room with the man.

Garth was over eighty years old. He was still as mean as they come. The attack on Trent and Darcey's family at the Pines a few days ago proved that.

Eventually the old man opened his eyes. When he spoke his voice was weak. Barely audible.

"You come to watch me die, Sheriff?" he said, trying to laugh but the sound coming from him was more like wheezing than laughter.

"I always thought you were too mean to die, Garth."

"Yeah, I know," the old man said, his voice almost a whisper. "At least I'm cheating you out of sending me to Angola to let 'em stick a needle in my arm."

185

"It's ironic, isn't it, Garth, that I could never pin anything on you until now," Blake said. "I finally had you when you ordered the attack on the Pines. And that's when your heart blew out."

"You might not believe this, Blake, but that thing at the Pines got way out of control," Garth said. "It was supposed to be only a diversion. There was another plan in place but it didn't happen."

"A diversion?" Blake was incredulous. "Your men attacked six of my deputies. One of my guys almost died. You call that a diversion?"

"Yeah, well, my oldest boy, Stuart, is a little excitable," Garth said. "He got carried away. One of your deputies sent a bullet through his voice box. He won't ever be able to talk again. And another of your men killed my youngest boy, Mackie."

"And Sterling surrendered," Blake added. "He's doing a lot of talking, Garth, trying to save his skin."

"Sterling never was the fighter the other two were."

"Who hired you, Garth?" Blake asked. "At least have the decency to tell me that before you die."

"Sorry, Jack," the old man said, his eyes slowly closing. "Can't do it. Can't change my ways now. Got to go soon. Mackie's waitin' for me."

Trent, Darcey, Christopher, and Nancy checked into suites at the Captain Cook hotel after the attack on the penthouse. After they all got some sleep, Darcey booked flights to San Francisco for Christopher and Nancy.

Their concern that their new neighbors might block the purchase of the penthouse was alleviated the next day as Trent and Darcey wandered through the detritus left from the fight. As they talked about the repairs Miles would oversee and Darcey described her plan for the new design of the penthouse, they were surprised to hear a voice behind them.

"You folks sure know how to make an entrance."

Trent and Darcey turned to find an elderly man standing just inside the open door.

Darcey found her voice first.

"We're very sorry about the disturbance, sir," she said. "I assure you it won't happen again."

"Well, if it does," the older man said, "you just give a shout and I'll come a'running. Me and my Paratrooper."

186

As he spoke, he revealed the vicious looking rifle he had been holding behind his back.

"Had this baby custom made," he said. "I was all set to come down here and lend a hand but you folks got things under control before I could get locked and loaded. I was a little disappointed. It was the most excitement I've had since I retired from the army."

He introduced himself as Clifford and his wife, who stood beside him, was Ethel. They lived in the other penthouse on the top floor of the building.

"And you don't have to worry about Ethel either," Clifford continued. "She's a soldier's wife. She can take care of herself."

To demonstrate Clifford's faith in his wife was well-placed, Ethel showed the Ruger semiautomatic she had been holding behind her back.

Clifford told Trent and Darcey not to worry about any of the other residents of the building.

"I did all right in real estate when I got out of the army," he explained. "I own the land this building is on. I still have enough influence to ward off any potential complaints. And when you folks aren't here, you needn't worry about anything. Ethel and I will keep an eye on your place."

The older couple had only one request.

"You people sure eat good," Clifford said. "There have been some mouthwatering aromas drifting over from your direction. We wouldn't mind being invited for dinner once in a while."

Christopher had to get back to work. His chief had been accommodating but he had been out of the office for far too long. It was time for him to get back to work as captain of homicide detectives.

Nancy flew home without knowing where her next job would be. When she went to her old precinct station to collect the personal items she hadn't bothered to take when she quit her job and stormed out, she was pleasantly surprised. Captain Terry Wooster, her old captain, the one whose men called the Rooster behind his back, had been asked to retire. He protested but quickly learned it wasn't really a request.

The man who was appointed to take his place asked Nancy to rescind her resignation and offered her a promotion to lieutenant as inducement to stay with the suburban police force. It was enough.

Robert was kept in the hospital for two days for observation. His wound was more painful than dangerous. He was lucky. He would be stiff and sore for a while but nothing vital was hit.

When he was released, he joined Trent and Darcey at the hotel. He walked with assistance from a cane but that was only temporary, the doctors assured him. His wound was on his right side so he leaned on the cane with his left hand.

Darcey poured flutes of Prosecco for the trio when cocktail hour arrived. They ordered dinner from room service.

Miles Diaz-Douglas was scheduled to fly in the next day. Darcey would spend a day with him going over their ideas for the penthouse. They planned to fly back to Louisiana the day after that.

Robert said he'd like to stay around for a few days if they didn't mind. He promised to join them for Christmas in the refurbished penthouse.

"The next time you decide we should take a vacation, Trent, we should consider something a little less exciting," Darcey said. "Maybe a weekend binge watching old movies with all the doors locked and the curtains drawn."

"You do have a knack for attracting adventure, Trent," Robert said, as he cut another bite from the huge, rare steak on his plate. "Even when he was a kid, Darcey, it was the same. His dad and I never knew what was going to happen when we traveled with the boy. We only knew it would be something out of the ordinary, usually involving a hungry bear or an angry moose and one extraordinarily frightening adventure with a wolverine. A wolverine has a nasty disposition even on his best day."

"At least it's all over now," Darcey said.

"Not quite," Robert said. "There's still one loose end we have to tie up."

He would say no more.

August 26th

Trent and Darcey spent Saturday at the Pines with their daughter, Betty, and Ivy. Kelli was so excited to see them after the long separation and the adventures of the summer. The little girl stayed by the side of at least one of them all day. Kelli's parents were every bit as happy to be with their daughter again.

Trent was still trying to absorb whatever it was he experienced while he was in the coma. Was it all hallucination? Were those who visited him the spirits of people in his life?

He tended to lean toward the latter. He couldn't explain why. They didn't feel like hallucinations. It didn't have to go beyond that. He remembered they said they didn't understand either. They said it wasn't necessary to understand.

It was warm but not uncomfortably so when cocktail hour arrived. They were gathered on the front porch enjoying the view, watching the horses cavorting in the pasture.

For the first time since early July, Trent did the honors. He mixed peach martinis for Darcey and himself, peach iced tea for Betty and Ivy, and peach nectar in a sippy cup for Kelli.

At Dr. Shannon's direction, the bandage on Trent's head had been removed. The hair was beginning to grow back but in a different color. There was a streak of silver where the bullet had interrupted normal growth.

"Sexy," Darcey said when she saw it.

They left the big Jeep at the Pines now. It was more fitting and useful for the rural parish when they visited the farm.

Since Trent had managed to collect an arsenal in San Francisco almost as extensive as the New Orleans gun room, they were flying back and forth more than driving. He left the Bentley in the secured parking garage of the Nob Hill Condo.

The Cadillac CTS-V was in New Orleans. It was much easier to wheel through the narrow streets of New Orleans than was the Jeep.

Darcey had bought a black Cadillac Escalade in Anchorage. Miles would use it while he was in town working on the penthouse. He would live in the caretaker's apartment while the work was being done.

He was already hiring subcontractors. He wanted the penthouse stripped and rebuilt by the end of September. The subcontractors were doubtful. Miles wasn't worried. They had never worked for anyone like him before. They would meet their deadlines. Since he hinted that DJA Designs would be opening an Anchorage office with lots of work for subcontractors, they were all anxious to impress him.

After Betty and Ivy took Kelli upstairs to bed, Trent poured a second peach martini for Darcey and himself. They sat contented on the wide front porch of the Pines.

"What was it like?" Darcey asked.

Trent looked at her. He didn't speak for long minutes.

"The worst of it was the humiliation," he said at last. He didn't look at her as he spoke. He stared over the pasture.

"When you are too weak to stand and have to be lifted onto a potty chair. When you're done and have to be held up by one nurse while another cleans you. There is nothing remaining of human dignity."

He sat silently again, drinking his martini. Trying unsuccessfully to forget.

"And the coma," she said. "What was it like being in the coma?"

"I can't explain it. Not even to myself. It was very confusing."

"You hear stories about people seeing a white light or hovering on the ceiling watching everyone in the room," she said.

"There was none of that. There were times when I knew you were there. I could hear you but couldn't respond," he said.

He hesitated. Darcey didn't push him.

"People visited me," he said, finally. "People long gone. My dad. My best friend since I was ten. Even my mother just as I was coming out of it. I couldn't speak or open my eyes but I saw them. I could communicate with them. They were all very pleasant. Except for one terrible night when Josh Blair showed up. That was very disturbing."

"Dr. Shannon said you appeared to have been quite agitated one night," she told him. "That must have been the night."

They were quiet for a while. He didn't tell her about the overwhelming wave of pinpricks that consumed him as he came out of the coma. That would come later.

"I can't explain it, Darcey. I don't really understand it."

He was silent for a while.

"They all said it wasn't necessary to understand. I only needed to believe. They all said that. Believe."

Hackett sat in the dark in the living room of his cheap duplex apartment in the rundown neighborhood. He was on his second vodka over ice and fully planned to pour a third.

He was waiting. Night after night following his return to Anchorage. He had waited.

It would come. Sooner or later it would come. He didn't doubt it.

It came tonight. The knock on the door.

"It's open, Robert," Hackett called out. "Come on in."

Robert Monk entered the room cautiously.

"I've been expecting you."

"I would have been here earlier but one of your friends required me to spend a couple of days in bed," Monk said.

"How did you figure it out?"

"It wasn't hard, James," Monk replied. "Had to think about it but you're the only one who made sense."

"There were cops in and out in New Orleans, Robert, and you know how many dirty cops are about," Hackett said, chuckling. "And then we arranged for the delivery guy to bring groceries in every day. I could posit it could have been the delivery guy."

"Yeah, the delivery guy was a good feint, James, but it didn't work when you guys went out to the farm. Greco still knew what was going on."

Hackett nodded.

"I knew you'd figure it out then," he said. "You know, I really liked that farm. Raquel and I wanted a place like that. We wanted to move to New Mexico when I retired."

"Life has a way of not working out the way we dream it," Monk said.

"Don't lecture me about life," Hackett said, suddenly belligerent.

"What happened, James? Why?"

"What happened?" Hackett was almost shouting. "You want to know why? Death happened, Robert. That's what happened. Raquel's death. I died with her. Everything died with her."

"Do you think she would have wanted this?"

"I don't know what she would have wanted, Robert," Hackett said, sounding now more miserable than angry. "She suffered. Oh, how she suffered. Did you know she begged me to kill her?

"What happened? All I know is one day she was gone and I was left with nothing. I had no money. Our home was repossessed. I was bankrupt and deep in debt. Had to sell my truck and buy that used piece of junk you see outside now."

"But you were an Alaska state employee. When you signed up we had the best insurance available anywhere. That should have covered her medical bills. Why did you go broke?"

"When the doctors here and in Seattle said there was nothing more they could do, I took six months off without pay. I traveled with Raquel to every doctor in every country I could find who promised they could cure her," Hackett said, bitterness framing every word. "Quacks. Every one of them. Nothing but quacks. Insurance didn't pay for them. They took nothing but cash. Every dollar I could lay my hands on."

"When did you go to work for Greco, James? How did you meet him?"

"Not long after he got here. Don't really remember how I met him. Couldn't afford to go to his restaurant. He came looking for me, I guess. He was good at figuring how who might be bought and how to buy them.

"At first it was small jobs. Mainly supplying him with information."

"Then the jobs got bigger?" Monk pursued.

"Yeah, Robert, then the jobs got real big. As big as they get."

Robert waited.

"He sent me to San Francisco for the first big job. One of his employees stole forty thousand from him. Greco wanted his money back and he wanted to set an example for his other employees. Wanted them to see what happened if they stole from him."

"The first one, James?" Robert asked, surprised.

"Yeah, there were others. One in Wyoming. Another in Kentucky."

Robert felt sick to his stomach listening to his old friend confess to multiple murders.

"And the two in New Orleans?"

"They were expendable," Hackett, emotionless. "I wouldn't let them get close to the house. They were intended only to flush us out from behind the brick wall. The world is better off without them."

"James, the old man who arranged the attack on the Pines told the sheriff it was supposed to be only a diversion," Robert said, not wanting to hear Hackett's reply.

"I wasn't going to kill them, Robert," Hackett protested. "I was supposed to sneak them out during the attack and get them to a cabin the old man had back out in the woods. Greco wanted me to hold them there to use for leverage if you or anybody else got too close to busting his operation."

"Why didn't you do it?"

"Because the whole thing was out of control," Hackett explained. "The old man's sons started shooting at the cops and the cops shot back. People were being hit. Being killed. There was no way I could get the women and that child safely out of the house."

"He would have ordered you to kill them sooner or later, James. You know that."

Hackett poured another glass of vodka. He drank half of it.

"Yeah, I know," he said. "But I wouldn't have done it, Robert. Really I wouldn't. I wouldn't have killed that little girl and those two women. I couldn't do that."

"I want to believe that, James."

"You can believe it. I couldn't do that."

Hackett downed the remainder of the vodka.

"You know, Robert, you've heard it said that your life flashes before your eyes just before you die," Hackett said. "It's true, you know, but they don't have it quite right."

Monk said nothing. He let Hackett talk.

"It doesn't happen quickly. It plays out in jerks and jumps and stops and starts. I've been seeing scenes from my life for years. I've relived every day since my first memory. I've seen replays of every mistake I ever made. They run through my mind like bad movies. I don't sleep much anymore. I just lie in bed watching the reruns of my life."

The two friends were quiet. There was nothing left to be said.

Hackett raised the snub-nosed Korth Sky Marshall revolver and fired. The bullet flew harmlessly over Monk's left shoulder. Hackett was an expert marksman with a handgun.

Robert Monk raised the Glock he was holding by his side. He was also an expert marksman. His bullet was true.

Now it was over.